EL SOLDADO

THE SOLDIER

ALSO BY WILLIAM C. DIETZ

LEGION OF THE DAMNED

Legion of the Damned
The Final Battle
By Blood Alone
By Force of Arms
For More Than Glory
For Those Who Fell
When All Seems Lost
When Duty Calls
A Fighting Chance
From the Ashes

ANDROMEDA (LEGION OF THE DAMNED PREQUEL SERIES)

Andromeda's Fall
Andromeda's Choice
Andromeda's War

THE MUTANT FILES

Deadeye
Redzone
Graveyard

AMERICA RISING

Into the Guns
Seek and Destroy
Battle Hymn

THE RUNNER DUOLOGY

Runner
Logos Run

THE SAURON DUOLOGY

*Deathday**
*Earthrise**

THE EMPIRE DUOLOGY

*At Empire's Edge**
*Bones of Empire**

THE CORVAN DUOLOGY

Matrix Man
Mars Prime

THE DRIFTER TRILOGY

Drifter
Drifter's Run
Drifter's War

THE McCADE SERIES

Galactic Bounty
Imperial Bounty
Alien Bounty
McCade for Hire†
McCade on the Run†

WINDS OF WAR

Red Ice
Red Flood
Red Dragon
Red Thunder
Red Tide
Red Sands
Red River
Red Dog

STANDALONE WORKS

Freehold
Prison Planet
Where the Ships Die
Bodyguard
The Seeds of Man
Rogan's World
Steelheart
Snake Eye
Ejecta

GAMING NOVELS & NOVELLAS

THE DARK FORCES TRILOGY (STAR WARS)

Soldier for the Empire
Rebel Agent
Jedi Knight

THE RESISTANCE DUOLOGY (STAR WARS)

The Gathering Storm
Resistance: A Hole in the Sky

OTHER GAMES

Halo: The Flood
Hitman: The Enemy Within
Heaven's Devils
Mass Effect: Deception

†Omnibus edition

EL SOLDADO

THE SOLDIER

WILLIAM C. DIETZ

JABberwocky Literary Agency, Inc.

Acknowledgments

I would like to thank Lisa Rodgers, who could have accepted *El Soldado* as it was, but chose to dive in and make it better. I will forever be thankful for her help.

To Wyatt,
Shoot straight, protect the weak, and police your brass.
Love, Papa

Prologue

U.S. State Department Travel Warning for Tampico, Mexico

"Tamaulipas (includes Matamoros, Nuevo Laredo, Reynosa, and Tampico): U.S. citizens should defer all non-essential travel to the state of Tamaulipas due to violent crime, including homicide, armed robbery, carjacking, kidnapping, extortion, and sexual assault.

The number of reported kidnappings in Tamaulipas is among the highest in Mexico. State and municipal law enforcement capacity is limited to nonexistent in many parts of Tamaulipas. Violent criminal activity occurs more frequently along the northern border and organized criminal groups may target public and private passenger buses traveling through Tamaulipas. These groups sometimes take all passengers hostage and demand ransom payments.

U.S. government personnel are subject to movement restrictions and a curfew between midnight and 6 a.m. Matamoros, Reynosa, Nuevo Laredo, and Ciudad Victoria have experienced numerous gun battles and attacks with explosive devices in the past year."

Chapter One

Uvalde, Texas

It was Nick Serrano's birthday. But, as he stared at the image in the mirror, there wasn't much to celebrate. The man who met his gaze had two days' worth of stubble, a .357 bullet dangling from a chain, and the words *Semper fi* tattooed on his chest. There were scars, too. The latest of which was still red and tender.

A few clothes, his guns, and a truck. That's what Serrano had to show for his 36 trips around the sun. There had been money in the bank once, but his woman took that, and spent it on another man. So, what to do?

Never give up. That's one of the many things Serrano had learned during eight in the Crotch. *Seize opportunities* was another.

Serrano checked his forty dollar Timex. It was 18:32 and time to go to work. And, assuming that Serrano had the stones, it was time to change his life for the better.

Serrano brushed his teeth, sprayed deodorant under both arms, and got dressed. His outfit consisted of a western style black shirt, jeans, and boots.

His rig included two holsters, one on his strong side for a S&W 7-shot revolver, and a cross draw for the pistol he thought of as *Shorty*, because of its three-inch barrel.

The belt and holsters were supported by leather suspenders, both equipped with cartridge loops, 7 on each side. All in .357 magnum. All street legal in Texas.

"The same ammo for every gun." That was Serrano's motto. And no semiautomatics. Not after Serrano's nine jammed in Syria, and damn near got him killed.

A Levi jacket went on over Serrano's arsenal and a cowboy hat settled onto his head. The rest of his stuff went into an AWOL bag. The room had been paid for in advance, which allowed Serrano to depart without visiting the office.

His Toyota Tundra pickup was lifted for offroad use. That made it easier to take a knee, grab the flashlight clipped to the frame, and check the vehicle's frame for bombs and trackers. Not because Serrano was expecting trouble, but because it was a good habit, like brushing his teeth. Then it was time for him to test the hood lock and inspect both doors for any signs of tampering. There weren't any.

Serrano was in Uvalde, west of San Antonio, so it made sense to get on 35. That took him to the outskirts of San Antonio, where Serrano paused to grab a Whopper, prior to reporting to his job as a guard. Not a security guard in a shopping mall. But a "guard," whose job it was to check on and, if necessary, to protect one of Mr. Yankovic's "collectors."

Serrano had been recommended for the job by an old Marine Corps buddy named Cory Dalton. He had explained that the job was part of a money laundering scheme.

"Basically, Mr. Yankovic and his posse steal crypto, process it via the blockchain, and dump it into a digital wallet. Then they move the crypto to a Bitcoin ATM, sell it, and take the cash. All before anyone has time to detect the scam and stop it.

"The collectors travel from ATM to ATM. The max is 10K

from each. That's why there are multiple collectors. A guard follows each collector to make sure they aren't robbed, and are present to witness the handoff to an aggregator. Meaning one of Yankovic's lieutenants. Each guard gets 500 smackers a day. Sweet, huh?"

It *was* sweet. Except for the fact that people were being robbed. An ethical dilemma that made Serrano feel uncomfortable. But hadn't stopped him from accepting the job.

After leaving the drive-thru Serrano drove to the parking lot where his collector was waiting. He flashed his high beams, received a response, and pulled into a slot.

Then it was time to scan the lot for potential hijackers while the collector entered the hotel. Serrano didn't see anything suspicious, so he managed to eat half his dinner before the collector reappeared with a slim briefcase in hand. *For the money*, Serrano decided, as he wiped his mouth.

Serrano followed the collector for three hours, as he traveled from place to place, and eventually wound up in a parking lot behind a church. A neon cross glowed above them.

A black Hummer was waiting. Lights flashed. Serrano's collector left his car—briefcase in hand.

This is it, Serrano told himself. *Put up or shut up*. He got out, long gun pressed against his right thigh, and ambled over to the Hummer.

The aggregator was an amateur weight lifter judging from his skin tight tee and thick arms. "You know the rules," the aggregator said. "Return to your truck. I'll pay you there."

Serrano brought the pistol up. "Drop to the ground and spread your arms. If you reach for a weapon, I'll shoot you."

The collector dropped. The aggregator didn't. "You're making a serious mistake," the weight lifter said. "If you steal from Mr. Yankovic, he'll track you down."

Serrano was in no mood to consider the future. "He'll try," Serrano said. "Now drop."

The aggregator obeyed.

The Taser X2 was ready in Serrano's left hand. He shot both men. They began to convulse as Serrano took the slim briefcase and made his way over to the Hummer, where a gym bag filled with cash was sitting on the passenger seat.

So far, so good, Serrano thought, as he carried the money to his truck. *It's time to haul ass.* Tires screeched as he left the lot.

Like many bandits before him, Serrano was headed for Mexico by way of the McAllen crossing. There were numerous reasons for that, the first and foremost of which was Serrano's dual American/Mexican citizenship, a gift from his divorced parents.

As a child, Serrano spent the winter months in the U.S., going to school, and doing what boys do. During summers Serrano supposedly lived with his dad in the town of Lugar de Paz. But, since his father was rarely there, it fell to his grandfather to help raise him.

And that was the second reason for fleeing to Mexico. Serrano wanted to visit Papá, even though his stay would be necessarily brief. The last thing Serrano wanted to do was bring Yankovic's thugs to Lugar de Paz. Such a thing wasn't certain of course. But Serrano couldn't take the chance.

Last and certainly not least was Serrano's hope that he could, with the help of Yankovic's cash, create a new identity for himself. The details of which hadn't been established.

It was a straight shot down Highway 281. Traffic was light that time of night, the air was cool enough to open a window, and the two-hour drive to the town of Alice was uneventful.

Serrano considered buying fuel there. But, with half a tank of gas, he decided to push the pit stop off to Falfurrias, where he would refuel, take a pee, and buy coffee.

Serrano took the exit for Falfurrias forty minutes later, pulled into a brightly-lit gas station, and took notice of a flatbed truck with a crew cab.

There was nothing remarkable about such a rig in south Texas. But the fact that it was parked off to one side, where three teenage boys were smoking what Serrano assumed to be marijuana, caught his attention.

Situational awareness. That's what noncoms emphasized in the Corps, and Serrano knew, because he'd been a staff sergeant. So, he marked the boys on his mental map, and went about his business. The teens were still goofing around when he left.

Serrano was about ten minutes into the one-hour drive to McAllen, when headlights became visible in his rearview mirror, and grew steadily brighter until a truck passed on the left. Serrano recognized it as the same flatbed he'd seen at the gas station.

Without warning, the truck cut in front of Serrano and braked. The distance between the vehicles was so short that Serrano couldn't avoid hitting the flatbed with his brush guard.

The maneuver was intentional, no doubt about that, so Serrano shifted into reverse. Suddenly headlights appeared from the rear, topped by red and yellow flashers. The police?

No, in spite of the glare, Serrano could see the outline of a tow truck.

It was a trap. Stop a driver, rob him, and steal his vehicle. Rather than be trapped in his truck, Serrano released his seat belt and opened the door.

A boy, probably late teens, was standing there, pistol in hand, aiming it at Serrano. The ex-marine shot him in the chest, and turned to shoot a second teen in the head, even as the tow truck's driver fired.

The bullet snapped past. Serrano ducked, fired, and saw the man fall.

The next bullet was in keeping with what Gunnery Sergeant Logan liked to say. "If the bastard is worth one, he's worth two."

That left the third teen. He was in the flatbed and planning to haul ass. And it would have worked if the flatbed's trailer hitch hadn't been tangled up in the Tundra's brush guard.

The kid was at the wheel, pedal to the metal, and going nowhere—when Serrano shot him through the side window. The impact threw him sideways and out of sight.

As for the other bodies, Serrano managed to drag them around to the shoulder of the road, before a semi roared past. Then, by jumping up and down on the Tundra's brush guard, Serrano managed to free it.

As for feelings of guilt, there were some, in spite of the fact that Serrano had been acting in self-defense. Perhaps Tupac Shakur put it best when he said, "…Live by the gun and die by the gun." The hijackers had made a choice and it was the wrong one.

Serrano pulled over about five miles short of the border, pressed a button under the dash, and watched the overhead tray whine down. Serrano had purchased the used Tundra from a company that specialized in armored vehicles, because he wanted something with T6 level protection, given all the crime in Mexico.

There was no way to know what the previous owner kept up there, but drugs were one possibility, as were weapons. And that's what Serrano had in mind.

His rifle and shotgun were already in the tray. So, all Serrano had to do was add the rig, plus Yankovic's cash, which fit in around the weapons. Once that chore was taken care of, Serrano raised the tray.

Could the customs officers find the stash? They not only could, but they would, if they chose to look. But Serrano felt sure that his red passport, the kind issued to officials and military personnel, would get him through.

Thanks to the early morning hour, the line was relatively short. Big rigs mostly, hundreds of which crossed the border every day.

But despite the short line, it still took halfan-hour starts and stops to advance to the island where a long-suffering customs agent was waiting. "Passport please."

Serrano felt a rising sense of apprehension as he handed the maroon-colored passport across. Was it still good? Or had one of the cube dwellers at the DOD cancelled it?

That would be legit after all, since Serrano was back from Venezuela, and off the black ops payroll. The agent looked from the passport photo to Serrano. "Welcome back Mr. Costas… How was the trip south?"

"About what you'd expect," Serrano replied.

"And you have business in Mexico?"

"Affirmative."

The agent handed the passport back. "Watch your six, Mr. Costas. And thank you for your service."

Serrano nodded. "And thank you for yours."

The Mexican checkpoint was on the other side of the McAllen-Hildago International Bridge in Reynosa. Thanks to the early hour, and nine southbound lanes, there was hardly any delay for Mexican nationals.

Serrano waited for an exhaust-spewing semi to clear the way, pulled forward, and proffered his Mexican passport. A real one this time, with two Grants tucked inside. "Buenos días."

The way Serrano looked, his coastal accent, and the "fee" were sufficient to establish his bonafides. The agent stamped a page and returned it.

"Bienvenido, señor."

As Serrano accepted the passport, he could tell that the fifties were missing. He smiled. It was good to be back.

Serrano's plan was to follow 85 south to Monterrey, check into a decent hotel, and get some serious Zs. It was a four-hour drive. And, by the time Serrano arrived, he was exhausted.

After purchasing some fast food, which he ate in the truck, Serrano checked into a chain hotel. His room was nice, but not exceptional. He threw a pillow into the crevasse between the queen-size bed and the wall, jerked the quilt free, and made a nest on the floor.

Then Serrano used extra pillows and a blanket to create what looked like a sleeping person on the bed. The purpose of which was to absorb bullets while Serrano returned fire, a trick that had worked in Belize City.

Then, with Shorty next to his hand, Serrano went to sleep. He awoke ten hours later. *I'm free*, Serrano thought. *Free from the Corps, free from the DOD, and free from Mr. Yankovic.* It felt good.

Breakfast was a big plate of huevos rancheros from room service. Serrano followed that with a hot shower, a shave, and a clean tee shirt. His last one.

Serrano used cash to pay for his room and a tank of gas. Dollars were okay at that point. But wouldn't work in smaller towns. That meant changing some as soon as possible.

After topping his tank Serrano hit the road. He was on 54, headed for Guadalupe.

Time passed. The sun was out, and Norteña music was play-ing on the radio, when Serrano passed through Concepción del

Oro—and entered the desert beyond.

Traffic was light, and Serrano was thinking about how surprised his grandfather would be, when flashing lights appeared in his rearview mirror. *Policía Federal.* Shit.

Was Serrano speeding? Yes. But only by the usual ten miles an hour. So why pull him over? Because the Federales were bored? Or because they wanted to "squeeze" an American? The truck had Texas plates after all.

Serrano pulled over, removed his wallet from a back pocket, and fumbled for the license. It was ready by the time the Federales ambled up cop style, one on each side of the truck, so they could see the cab's interior.

And that was a good idea, except that they were in each other's line of fire. "You were driving over the limit," the officer on the driver's side said, as he accepted Serrano's license.

The cop was speaking English, on the assumption that the American didn't speak Spanish, so Serrano decided to go the home boy route. "Tenía los ojos puestos en la carretera, oficial, así que no vi el velocímetro."

It was a joke and another policeman might have laughed. This one frowned. "Your license has expired."

That was true. Serrano's Mexican license had expired while he was stuck in Venezuela's El Rodeo Prison, fighting to stay alive. Serrano realized that he should have offered the American equivalent instead.

Serrano was about to provide it, when a pickup loaded with gunmen screeched to a stop and opened fire with assault weapons. They were firing entire magazines instead of three-round bursts. Amateurs then.

The cop next to Serrano was killed instantly. The other one drew his sidearm and was hiding behind the Tundra when the gun truck pulled around to fire on him as well.

Serrano wanted to leave the scene but couldn't. His driver's license was outside, lying on the ground, and when the police found it—they'd assume that he'd been involved in the murders.

Even if Serrano wasn't bulletproof the Tundra was. So, it was tempting to sit and wait the bandoleros out. But Serrano had a strong desire to retrieve the license and disengage before more people came along. So, he freed himself from the seatbelt, opened the door, and rolled onto the pavement.

The ID card was right there, just inches from the dead cop's fingers. Serrano grabbed it and crawled under the Tundra as bullets chipped the concrete in front of him.

The long .357 and its snap-off holster were resting on the passenger seat. But Serrano had Shorty to work with, and plenty of people to shoot at. After scooting out from the pickup's safe side, Serrano fired at a succession of targets. So many that it was necessary to pause and reload using a moon clip.

That was when one of the forajidos got into the pickup and stomped on the gas. The truck bounced as it rolled over a wounded bandido, and probably killed him.

Serrano had to circle around in order to enter the Tundra. He swore when he saw all the bullet blisters on the windshield, then took off.

The scene in the rearview mirror was a horror show. The cop car was sitting there, lights flashing, surrounded by bodies.

At that point Serrano figured the policemen had been on the up and up, and were murdered for that reason, which sucked.

And because one of the forajidos had escaped, a description of the Tundra was jumping from cellphone to cellphone by then, as the survivor called on other gang members to watch for the pistolero responsible for so many deaths.

Serrano put his foot down, felt the truck surge ahead, and

hoped to reach Guadalupe in record time. Or, was that stupid? The bad guys would cruise Highway 54, guns loaded, looking for a shot-up Tundra. And, they might use drones, too.

So, what other options were there? Serrano knew that the turnoff for Estevez was coming up. It was a secondary route that would take Serrano to Lugar de Paz, via a twisting-turning country road. But that was okay given the circumstances.

Serrano braked, and had to wait for a dump truck loaded with two-man rocks to pull out onto Highway 54, before taking a left and heading east. Along the way he passed a bus stop with a faded plywood roof and adjoining skeletal tree. Beautiful, it wasn't.

The subsequent two-hour journey took Serrano past a rock quarry and up and over a series of barren hills, before descending into sunbaked Estevez.

It consisted of a convenience store, a laundromat, a hardware store, a barber shop and a single restaurant—Las Palmeras. Although all that remained of the palm trees were some stumps.

Serrano didn't dare stop. People knew people in towns like Estevez. And word of the shootout on Highway 54 could have reached there already. No, it was best to pass through, and hope to escape notice.

Serrano crossed the steel bridge that led into Lugar de Paz forty-five minutes later. The sign emblazoned with the town's name was riddled with bullet holes.

Chapter Two

San Antonio, Texas

Mr. Yankovic wasn't happy. And when Mr. Yankovic wasn't happy, neither were the people around him. Not his mistress, not his bodyguards, and definitely not the aggregator strapped to the stainless steel gyno table. The drops of blood that dripped from the aggregator's crotch caused a pinging sound as they hit the metal basin below.

The aggregator's name was Max, and he'd been able to make it all the way to Tucson, before bodyguards Huey and Dewey tracked him down.

Yankovic had a tall crewcut, permanent bags under his eyes, and a determined mouth. "So," Mr. Yankovic said. "You ran. Yet, according to your story, it was this Nick Serrano character who took the cash."

"Y-y-yes, sir," Max stuttered.

"Then why run?" Yankovic demanded.

"I-I-I knew you'd be upset."

"Like I am now."

"Y-y-yes."

Mr. Yankovic turned to Louie. "You know what to do. Oh, and send for Leo Creedy."

*

Lugar de Paz, Mexico

Memories of Serrano's youth came flooding back as he cruised past the old cinema, the barbershop where Papá took him, and the garage where he worked part time during the summers.

That was when Serrano spotted Father Colon. He was still tall, but stooped, as if carrying a great weight on his shoulders. The cleric had a cloth shopping bag clenched in each hand as he walked toward the church.

Serrano pulled over and rolled the passenger window down. A honk was required to get Colon's attention. The priest stopped, looked, and looked again. "Nicholas… Is that you?"

"It is," Serrano said. "Jump in… I'll take you home."

Colon opened the door, placed his groceries on the floor, and got in. Serrano pulled away from the curb. "Someone shot at you," Colon said matter of factly.

"Yeah," Serrano agreed. "They did."

Colon eyed him. "Have you been to La Casa Bonita?"

"No, I just arrived."

"What's it been?" Colon inquired. "Two years?"

"Three, Father. I used to work for the United States government. You know that. What you don't know is that I was on a helicopter, flying over Venezuela, when government forces shot it down. I woke up in a two-man cell occupied by five rebs. It took the DOD a long time to get me out."

"We must talk," the priest said. "There are many things you need to know. You will come into the church."

It was a command rather than an invitation. And Serrano wasn't about to tell the priest *no*.

The sun was starting to set as the men entered the Church of John the Warrior through the side door. Colon deposited his groceries on the kitchen counter and paused.

"You can wear your guns here, but not in the nave. Understood?"

"Understood," Serrano replied.

Colon led Serrano back to the Rectory. An oil painting of Jesus hung on one wall, a large desk was positioned in front of the windows, and a floor-to-ceiling bookcase occupied most of the third wall. "Please," Colon said, as he indicated the chairs positioned on opposite sides of a small table. "Have a seat."

Serrano chose the one that put his back to the bookcase, and allowed him to see both the windows and the door.

"First," Colon said, as he sat on the other chair. "You must prepare yourself for some bad news."

Serrano felt a sudden rush of sorrow. Papá was dead. He could see it on the priest's face. "When did Papá die? And how?"

"About six months ago," Colon replied. "He died of cancer. He tried to reach you. I tried to reach you. Nothing worked."

Serrano stared at the table top. "The prison guards used to bring letters to my cell, show me who they were from, and light them on fire."

Colon nodded. "That explains it. Your grandfather predicted this. 'My Nick will come home when he can.' That's what he said.

"I have the letter he wrote to you, and the deed for La Casa Bonita, which is yours now. Rosa and Emilio Morales have been caring for it.

"And in keeping with your grandfather's request, I've been paying them out of the funds he gave me. I hope you'll continue to employ them. They need the money."

"I will," Serrano promised. Which reminded him of Mr. Yankovic's money. He would have to hide it.

"Good," Colon said. "St. Augustine said, 'Without charity the rich man is poor...' When was your last confession?"

"More than three years ago," Serrano answered.

"Then you're overdue," Colon said sternly. "Let's begin."

Serrano bowed his head and made the sign of the cross. "Bless me Father for I have sinned. My last confession was more than three years ago.

"Since then, I killed three men while in prison, plus at least half a dozen more during the last 48 hours.

"I blasphemed thousands of times, I committed gluttony after my release from prison, and I felt hatred for those who imprisoned me.

"I lied, I viewed pornography, and I masturbated. Oh, and I stole money. A lot of it.

That's all I can remember. I'm sorry for my sins. Except for the killings. They deserved it."

Colon stared at Serrano. "That's quite a list my son. Perhaps the longest I've heard. As for who should die, only God can determine that."

"Yes, father."

"So," the priest added, "you must perform an act of penance. One that's commensurate to your long list of sins."

"Yes, father."

"Your penance will be to protect Lugar la Paz from evil," Colon said, as he made the sign of the cross. "Nothing more. And nothing less."

Serrano remembered the sign riddled with bullet holes. "That's likely to be a tall order, Father."

"Yes, it will be," Colon agreed. "Now you will say an Act of Contrition."

The words came slowly at first, but soon began to flow:

"My God,
I am sorry for my sins with all my heart.

In choosing to do wrong
and failing to do good,
I have sinned against you
whom I should love above all things.
I firmly intend, with your help,
to do penance,
to sin no more,
and to avoid whatever leads me to sin.
Our Savior Jesus Christ
suffered and died for us.
In his name, my God, have mercy."

"You remembered," Colon said, as he stood. "Solid proof that there is a God! You will park your truck behind the church, bring your suitcase in here, and sleep in my guestroom. If it's good enough for the bishop, it's good enough for you.

"I will phone Señora Morales and arrange for her to meet with us tomorrow morning."

Serrano did as he was told. The guest room had a window with a blind. A crucifix was mounted over the bed, a wardrobe was centered on a wall, and a chair was positioned next to a standing lamp. Serrano examined the envelope. His name was written with the block letters Papá had been trained to use during his time in the navy.

Serrano cut the envelope open, rather than tear it, and removed a single sheet of paper.

Dear Nick,

I haven't heard from you in years. Friends tell me to give up. They say you're dead.

But I know better. You are alive! And when you come, trouble will follow.

Protect the weak, and rely on Bruno. He will assist you.
I love you, son… And I will see you in heaven.

Papá

A tear fell on the word "Papá" and caused it to blur.

Serrano considered sleeping on the floor, but decided against it. *If I die in bed, then so be it,* he decided. *I need a good night's sleep. And I'm not likely to get it on a tile floor.*

Serrano thought he'd have a hard time getting to sleep but that wasn't the case. He awoke to find that sunlight was filtering in through the yellowing shade.

Serrano showered in what was obviously Father Colon's bath, shaved, and emerged to smell what turned out to be huevos a la Mexicana.

"Let's talk about your truck," Colon said. "I trust that you didn't buy it that way."

"No," Serrano agreed, as he forked eggs into his mouth. "I didn't."

"Did anyone other than you survive the fight?"

"Yes, Father. One bandido."

"Then his gang is looking for you. And the truck is a dead giveaway. We'll take it to Carlos Alonso. He'll fix the dings to the extent that's possible, and repaint it."

"He was a good guy," Serrano said. "Is that still the case?"

"Of course it is," Father Colon replied irritably. "Would I suggest him if he wasn't?"

There was no answer for that. So, after bringing the rest of his belongings inside, Serrano drove to the garage. Colon told him to park behind the building and he did. Alonso was wiping his hands with a greasy rag as he approached.

"Nick! Holy shit, it's you!"

The men embraced. They'd been on the same soccer team as youngsters.

"There is no such thing as 'holy shit,'" Colon put in.

"The two of you can grab a beer later." He eyed Alonso. "Nick needs to replace the windshield, fill in the dings, and paint it. What would that cost?"

Alonso circled the Tundra and returned. "Fifteen hundred U.S."

"Agreed," Colon said, without consulting Serrano. "In the meantime, Nick would like to rent something low key. Can you help with that?"

"Absolutely," Alonso replied. "I've got an old sedan in the back. Ten per day."

"Done," the priest said, as he extended his hand. "The keys, please. And hide the Tundra."

Ten minutes later, Serrano and Colon were driving away in a dusty 2015 Taurus which, according to Alonso, was equipped with a twin-turbocharged EcoBoost V-6 engine.

Serrano was behind the wheel and didn't need any guidance to find his way up the zigzagging road that led to La Casa Bonita. The two-bedroom, one bath home was similar to those around it.

But what made La Casa Bonita special was its high, red tile roof, bright-white paint job, window boxes filled with colorful flowers—and the carefully maintained wrought iron fence.

"You see?" Father Colon inquired. "Rosa and Emilio are taking good care of your home."

A home! Serrano had a home. That was amazing after all the years of living out of a duffle bag, followed by three years in a crowded jail cell. It felt good.

A VW Beetle was parked in the driveway. Serrano pulled in next to it.

Marigolds lined both sides of the drive.

When Serrano knocked on the door, Rosa opened it. She was fifty something, plump, and wearing what might have been her best dress. "¡Buenos días, señor Serrano! Y bienvenido a casa."

The hug felt natural, and Father Colon collected one as well. "I'm dusting," Rosa proclaimed. "Please let me know if you need anything."

"I will," Serrano said. "Thank you for taking care of the house after my grandfather's death. I hope you'll continue to do so. And Emilio too."

Colon smiled approvingly, and Rosa beamed. "Gracias, señor."

"You're welcome," Serrano replied. "If it's okay with you two, I'm going to look around. I have fond memories of this place."

"Of course," Father Colon said. "Take your time. Rosa and I have a church dinner to discuss."

Serrano's tour began in the living room. The ceiling was higher than most, with exposed rafters. A well-executed painting of a Spanish dancer, skirt twirling, hung over the fireplace. And Papá's favorite chair sat nearby.

A color photo of Serrano wearing his dress blue uniform hung on the wall next to the fireplace. *I look so young*, Serrano thought. *So innocent. Well, not anymore.*

Strangely, there were no pictures or other memorabilia related to Nick's father, Sergio Serrano. The man who deserted his wife and two-year-old son, for what? No one knew.

Serrano's room was much as he'd left it. The posters were gone. But the desk was there. Along with his now outdated computer. There were photos too. Serrano playing soccer. Serrano at the lake. And Serrano standing next to his first car.

Papá's room was frozen in time as well. A sombrero was hanging on a hook. An acoustic guitar stood on a stand in the corner. And there, dangling from a bedpost, was a holstered Colt .45. Serrano checked to see if the pistol was loaded. It was. As it should be.

"What good is an unloaded gun?" Papá liked to ask, whenever the subject of gun safety arose. "Will the desperados give me time to load?"

As Serrano held the gun in his hand, he remembered the lessons at the old quarry. Draw, aim, fire. Over and over again. It had gotten boring after a while.

But the practice paid off. Eventually, he applied to the USMC Shooting Team and was accepted. Handguns were Serrano's specialty, especially since he was ambidextrous and equally lethal with either hand. But he was good with long guns too. Good enough to be a sniper.

Serrano's thoughts were interrupted as Father Colon rushed into the room. "I got a call! Some pandilleros entered town—they've checked the garage and found the truck. They're holding Carlos hostage. They want you!"

Serrano returned the .45 to its holster. It was *his* fault. "Then let's provide them with what they want."

Colon was at the wheel as the Taurus careened down the hill and into town. "Will the police respond?" Serrano inquired.

The priest laughed. "Officer Molina? Not a chance. He works for El Cuchillo (The Knife). The man who runs the local cartel."

Serrano wanted to ask about Cuchillo and the cartel, but there wasn't enough time. Colon brought the car to a screeching halt a block from the garage.

"Stay here," Serrano advised. He then got out and made his way forward. The town was preternaturally quiet, except for the croaking sound produced by a Tamaulipas crow and the insistent ringing of a phone.

Once Serrano was close enough to be heard, he took cover behind a section of adobe wall, and cupped his hands. "This is Nick Serrano. I hear you're looking for me."

"Hell yes, I'm looking for you," a voice answered. "You killed my brother! Drop your weapons and walk in. Otherwise, the mechanic dies."

"Okay," Serrano said, as he lowered the gun rig to the ground. "I'm coming in."

The entrance to the garage was wide open. But it was difficult to penetrate the gloom. *Close,* Serrano thought. *I need to get close.*

"Raise your hands!" a bandit demanded. "Palms out."

Serrano raised his hands, confident that the bandits wouldn't notice the tiny aluminum sphere, or the rod attached to it.

Once inside the garage, Serrano could see them. Carlos was bleeding from his nose, his hands were tied behind his back, and his gaze was defiant. "Sorry, Nick...Your truck isn't ready yet."

A bandido pistol-whipped the mechanic, causing the others to turn their heads.

Serrano raised his left arm and used his fingers to press the ball twice. The spring-loaded derringer shot out of Serrano's sleeve, and into the palm of his hand.

Serrano couldn't risk headshots with such an inaccurate weapon. So, he fired at a torso, felt the recoil, and heard a loud *boom* as the .358 magnum bullet put the forajido on his ass.

Then it was time to switch targets. The second man was in motion, trying to aim, when Serrano shot him in the chest. The impact threw the outlaw backwards and onto the grease-stained floor.

Serrano waited to die. The math was simple. Two barrels, two bullets, three men. Game over.

Or it would have been over, had it not been for Carlos, soccer player that he was, who kicked the surviving gunman in the right knee.

That was the break Serrano needed. A large tool chest stood to his right. Serrano sent it rolling at the third man, who fired wildly.

Serrano bent to scoop a pistol off the floor. Two slugs from the 9mm put the last cabrón down for good.

Serrano helped Carlos to his feet. "That was a nice move, amigo. You saved my ass."

Townspeople were crowding in by then. "Come on," Serrano said. "Let's load the bodies into the Tundra, grab some beers, and head for the quarry. We'll have a bonfire. Truck and all."

Martina Blanco was pulling weeds in the vegetable garden, when she heard the shots, and hurried to grab the AR-15 that was leaning on the fence.

But there had been no text message warning the town's guerillas, most of whom were female, that an attack was underway. And, if El Cuchillo's scum were staging a raid, the gunfire would be nearly continuous. Four shots were meaningless.

Satisfied that nothing was amiss, Martina had returned to pulling weeds again when her friend Carmen arrived. "Did you hear? Three bandidos came to town and took Carlos hostage! Then Antonio Serrano's grandson arrived, and killed them all! And he's handsome."

"Good," Martina said. "You handle the gossip… And I'll take care of the vegetables."

But in spite of what Martina had said to Carmen, she was interested. A man who killed three bandidos by himself! He would be worth recruiting.

Chapter Three

Phoenix, Arizona

Leo Creedy was of the opinion that the hardest part of killing someone was finding them. Not always. But often. Nick Serrano was no exception. Especially since it looked as though his personal history had been wiped by professionals.

Why? Because he worked for some sort of heavy-duty criminal enterprise? Or for the government? The two being one and the same, to Creedy's way of thinking.

Facebook? Nada. Data scraping companies? Zero. People searches? Nope. But public records? Yes, in that Serrano had married Valerie Carter four years earlier in Texas and subsequently divorced.

Were they still in touch? Odds are that they were, for legal reasons if nothing else. So, if Creedy could find Valerie, chances were that he'd be able to find her thieving husband too.

Unlike Nick, Valerie was all over the social media sites, posing in a variety of skimpy clothing—and apparently bent on becoming an influencer.

But even though the thirty-something blond was pretty, could Val compete with eighteen-year-olds? Creedy didn't think so. Not that it mattered. Not that he really cared.

The recon mission was simple: Fly to Phoenix, the city that appeared in Val's social media posts, and have a chat with her.

But simple things can get complicated in a hurry. Especially given the professional manner in which Nick Serrano had neutralized two members of Mr. Yankovic's staff.

So, when Creedy boarded the plane for Phoenix, he was accompanied by two sidekicks, who had worked with him before. Boz was white, and Trev was black, consistent with Creedy's commitment to diversity.

Creedy and his two sides sat by themselves, didn't chat with the people around them, and were very courteous. A black ops vehicle was waiting for them. The rental rate was one thousand per day, and no wonder, since it was armored and untraceable. Payment was upfront in cash. But Creedy didn't give a shit. Mr. Yankovic was footing the bill.

The first step upon arrival was to latch onto Valerie Serrano and follow her home. And, thanks to all the marketing hype Val had posted, Creedy knew where to find her—at the Arizona Center Mall. There she, and half a dozen other "models," were scheduled to strut their stuff in front of a clothing store.

All Creedy and his sides had to do was hang out there, take notice when the MC called for Val to walk the walk, and wait for the event to end.

That was easy. Following Valerie to her car was more difficult than it should have been, because it took her a long time to pop in and out of stores, increasing the chances that she'd notice one or more of her stalkers.

Eventually, when Valerie entered the parking garage, the others stayed back, allowing Boz to tail her alone. The trick was timing. The side couldn't place the tracker on Val's ride until he knew which one was hers.

Boz knew that most people are distracted when they open a car door, slide inside, and fasten their seat belt. And Valerie was no exception.

So that was when the hitman increased his pace, paused long enough to attach the package to Valerie's rear bumper, and walk away.

An adhesive held the tracker in place rather than a magnet, since so many bumpers were made of plastic. A development Boz disapproved of.

After that it was easy to follow Valerie to a supermarket, then home to a development full of lookalike houses, and desert landscaping.

Creedy was planning to ring Valerie's doorbell and bullshit his way in, but that wasn't necessary. An alley ran behind the houses on Val's block, providing residents with the "gotta have" two car garages, which set the development apart from many others.

Valerie was exiting her Benz when a car stopped behind hers, two men got out, and grabbed her. Val opened her mouth to scream, and as she did so, Creedy stuffed a handkerchief into the hole. Valerie kicked futilely as she was lifted up off the ground, and carried into the pool area, where a young man in a Speedo was lying on a chaise lounge.

He started to get up, but fell back when Creedy shot him with a suppressed Ruger .22. One bullet to the head, and one to the torso.

The subsonic bullets made a soft *popping* noise. And, small though the slugs were, they were equal to the job. Valerie attempted to cry out but the improvised ball gag prevented her from doing so.

The door was unlocked. Creedy and Trev hustled Val into the kitchen, dumped her on top of the island she was so proud of, and used strips of duct tape to secure her limbs.

"There," Creedy said, as he removed the soggy handkerchief from Valerie's mouth. "I'm looking for you husband. Where is he?"

"I-I-I don't know," Valerie stuttered. "We're divorced."

"Okay," Creedy said. "Where do you think he is?"

"San Antonio?" Val inquired hopefully.

"We looked there," Trev put in.

"That's right," Creedy said. "We looked there. So, if your ex had to run, where would he go?"

Valeries's eyes darted from face-to-face. "Lugar de Paz," she said. "It's a town in Mexico. That's where his grandfather lives."

Creedy said, "Thanks," and shot Valerie in the head.

Lugar de Paz, Mexico

Three days had passed since the confrontation in the garage. And Serrano, at Father Colon's urging, was about to attend a church dinner. The sun was setting as people streamed past the church, under an arch, and onto a patio. Serrano followed.

Christmas style lights were draped between poles, buffet tables were heaped with food, and the crowd was festive. Except for one thing: At least half of the congregants were armed. Women included.

Serrano asked Carlos about that when the mechanic emerged from the crowd. "Ah yes, amigo. Have you noticed that there aren't any narcos hanging around town? That's because of the guerillas. Women mostly. But some men too... Who stand ready to fight El Cuchillo's bastardos if they try to take over."

"Why would they do that?"

"To steal, rape, and kidnap," Father Colon said, as he approached. "Nick... I would like to introduce Martina Blanco."

Martina had long black hair, an oval shaped face, and big eyes. She had something else as well, and that was charisma. "*El Soldado*," Martina said. "That's what they call you. Are you a soldado? Or, are you a pistolero?"

The challenge in Martina's voice was obvious. Colon smiled.

"I *was* a soldado," Serrano answered. "A sergeant in the United States Marine Corps. But not anymore."

"Will you teach us?" Martina demanded. "Or sit in the sun and watch us die?"

"That's enough, Martina," Father Colon said. "Do you want Nick's help? Or do you want to piss him off?"

Carmen arrived at that point. "Martina! They're waiting for you!" Martina allowed herself to be towed away.

"Martina is in charge of our guerilla fighters," Colon explained. "And she's quite passionate about it. Her husband was killed by the narcos eight years ago."

The priest might have said more, but was interrupted by a voice that boomed through the sound system. "Damas y caballeros... ¡Por favor, junten las manos por Martina Blanco!"

People began clapping as a mariachi band joined the crowd, and an improvised spot light found Martina as she began to sing *Tu Solo Tu* in a warm, full-bodied mezzo-soprano voice.

Serrano stood transfixed as Martina sang the love song, lost in the clarity of her voice and the depth of her emotion.

Loud applause followed the performance, and Serrano saw that a sombrero was making the rounds, and dropped a twenty into the hat as it passed by.

Then Father Colon took the mike, thanked Martina, and urged people to eat.

The rest of the evening was a blur. And, when Serrano drove home, he was thinking about Martina rather than the repairs Father Colon was hoping to fund.

The next day dawned gray, with low lying clouds in the west, and a distant mutter of thunder. After a simple breakfast of coffee, toast and bacon, Serrano drove down to the Día de la Independencia ballpark.

In spite of the important sounding name, the all-purpose ballpark wasn't much to look at. There were soccer nets at both ends of the mostly dirt field, with a scruffy baseball diamond in the middle, bracketed by weather-worn wooden seats.

Spectators were seated here and there, oldsters mainly, who were there to oversee the children playing all around them.

Approximately 50 people were doing calisthenics at center-field, led by none other than Martina Blanco, who was clearly in good shape. Her voice was loud enough to be heard on and off the field. "Come on! Ten more… You can do it!"

Serrano was carrying Shorty in a cross-draw holster, and was dressed in a t-shirt, shorts, and running shoes as he joined the group. Once Serrano started doing pushups, he realized that he needed to do them, and made a personal promise to work out every day.

When Martina called a halt, Serrano heard his name. "We have a new member!" Martina announced. "A person you've heard of, even if you haven't met him. His name is Nick Serrano. He's Antonio Serrano's grandson, and the man called *El Soldado*. He's going to advise us."

The announcement produced loud applause. Like Father Colon, Martina had a way of locking people in, and doing so without seeking their permission.

Serrano raised a hand by way of acknowledgement, even as Martina invited him to come forward. "So," Martina said. "What do you think of our guerillas now?"

"I think I'll take the rest of the day off." That drew laughs as it was supposed to.

"Someone has been eating too many burritos," Martina suggested tartly. "I would like our officers and noncoms to join Nick and me after we complete our laps. I want to pepper him with questions, and I'm sure you feel the same way."

Much to Serrano's chagrin he was winded after two laps around the field and happy to sit on a patch of grass for the impromptu meeting.

During the ensuing give-and-take, a number of things became clear. About 40 of the 52 members of the guerrilla force were women because they were effectively single, or their men were working, some far from home.

The trickle down from that was that the guerillas were more of a quick reaction force than a standing unit. And if a child was ill, and no one was available to babysit, individual guerillas felt free to ignore alerts.

Furthermore, officers and noncoms were elected, rather than being selected, which meant popularity was more important than proficiency.

And those were just the personnel issues. The unit was short of every kind of supply imaginable. Especially weapons and ammo.

Once the session was over, and parents went off to claim their children, Martina and Serrano had an opportunity to talk privately. "We're pretty messed up, huh?" Martin inquired.

"You fought El Cuchillo off," Serrano replied. "That's what Father Colon told me. That's a big deal."

"It is a big deal," Martina agreed. "But we were lucky. The narcos didn't expect any resistance. Not so much as a single shot. That was because Officer Molina didn't take our training sessions seriously. El Cuchillo cut him for that. That's the rumor.

"But even with the advantage of surprise we lost five people," Martina added. "We can't sustain those kinds of losses. You were a sergeant in the American Army?"

"The Marine Corps," Serrano replied.

"And that's better?"

"Marines think so," Serrano answered.

"So, Sergeant," Martina said. "What should I do?"

"Gradually transition away from elected leaders," Serrano suggested. "And break your squads down into four-person fire teams, each having a leader who can be promoted to sergeant if they prove themselves. Their subordinates will include an automatic rifleman, an assistant, and a rifleman."

"We have one fully automatic weapon," Martina countered.

"For now," Serrano replied. "We'll work on that. Plus, other necessities. And, once we get them, we'll have the right structure in place. Which is to say an organization that can be broken down into small, agile teams." He paused, and looked at Martina carefully. There were so many things to correct. Which one should he emphasize? "Right now I'm most concerned about your early warning system. How does it work? "Poorly," Martina confessed. "If someone sees something they think is suspicious, they phone or text me."

"Maybe you can recruit some old people to serve as lookouts," Serrano suggested. "Then we'll train them."

Their eyes locked. "So," Martina said. You'll help us."

"Yes."

"Why?" Her eyes were searching Serrano's face.

Serrano paused for a second. "Because my grandfather told me to."

Thunder rumbled in the distance and rain began to fall. It felt warm. Like newly spilled blood.

Leo Creedy hit paydirt in the local cantina. All he had to do was buy a drink for a drunk and tell him a lie. "I'm supposed to deliver a package to Señor Serrano. Can you tell me where he lives?"

"Sure," the drunk replied. "He lives in La Casa Bonita up on Beacon Hill."

"Beacon? How so?"

"Settlers used to light off a pile of brush when Comanches were coming," the man said. "It's the only hill in Lugar de Paz. You can't miss it."

Creedy left the cantina and returned to the black SUV. He had three sides with him, including Boz and Trev.

Creedy opened the front passenger door and got in. Boz was at the wheel. "We'll drive by the location," Creedy told him. "And ID the house. Then we'll go to dinner. I'm hungry."

It was dark by the time the crew finished dinner and made their way out of the restaurant to the parking lot. Beacon Hill was easy to find. And thanks to the scouting trip earlier that day, they knew which house belonged to Serrano.

"Oz," which was short for Ozborne, was an ex-locksmith. So, he went first, satchel in hand.

There weren't any lights, suggesting that Serrano was in bed, or elsewhere. In which case, the crew would enter and wait for him to return.

Serrano was dreaming about Martina. They were on a beach somewhere, and about to kiss, when something woke him. A sound? Yes, but *what* sound?

Suddenly the lights came on. A man was pointing a pistol at the bed. "Serrano! Wakey, wakey. Let me see your hands."

Serrano was lying on the floor as usual. He raised the long-barreled .357 and shot the intruder in the head. A mixture of blood and brains splattered the wall.

Serrano rolled under the old-fashioned bed in time to see a pair of fancy cowboy boots enter the room. He fired, the hitman fell, and a second bullet finished him off.

That was when a *third* killer launched himself through the air, landed on the bed, and began to fire down through the mattress. A bullet passed within an inch of Serrano's head.

That was a mistake. Serrano pressed his weapon against the sagging mattress and fired three times. He heard the hitman cry out, and elbowed his way back toward the sleeping bag.

A voice called to him. "Well, well... I'm impressed. Too bad we're on different teams. I could use a man like you."

Serrano was painfully aware of the fact that six of his pistol's seven rounds had been expended. And, if he could stall, he would. "Yankovic sent you to get his money... How much would you charge to simply walk away?"

Serrano was out from under the bed by then. Papá's Colt .45 was hanging from a bed post. Serrano stood, pulled the revolver free, and faced the door.

"Now you're talking," the hitman said. "A hundred thou. That's my price."

Serrano didn't believe it. And wasn't about to pay in any case. He threw the S&W out into the living room.

Serrano heard the *pop, pop, pop* of a suppressed .22 as the other man fired. Then he slipped through the doorway, pistol raised.

In order to survive, the hitman had to shift his aim from the S&W to Serrano in less than two heartbeats. He failed. The Colt produced a loud boom, as the .45 hollow point slug struck the intruder's right arm, and nearly severed it.

Blood pumped onto the tile floor as the hitman looked at it, attempted to keep his balance, and failed. There was a thump as the body hit the floor. Leo Creedy was dead.

Chapter Four

Lugar de Paz, Mexico

In another time, in another place, the attempt to kill Serrano would have caused a stir. But not in the Place of Peace. That was because Serrano's home had clearly been attacked, most of the dead men were gringos, and Mayor Aguilar, never mind Officer Molina, didn't want to get crosswise with an American gang. They already had El Cuchillo to deal with.

There were some winners however, including coffin maker Jorge Gómez, and undertaker Tomás Pérez. They were understandably neutral where murders were concerned.

As for death rites, there was only one flavor in Lugar de Paz, and that was Catholic. And Father Colon, who was by no means neutral, managed to condense the vigil, mass and committal into a single five-minute service attended by no one other than a black crow.

Meanwhile, Serrano and Emilio were working to clean the blood off La Casa Bonita's walls and floors. And once that was accomplished, to plaster over bullet holes, and apply two coats of paint.

That's what Serrano was doing when Martina arrived with a little boy and a Chihuahua. "Hi Nick, I'd like to introduce my son, Paco. He's eight. Shake hands with Señor Serrano, son."

Serrano extended his hand. "Hello, Paco… It's a pleasure to meet you."

Paco muttered something that was too soft to hear. "Paco's shy," Martina said. "He'll talk your ears off once he gets to know you.

"Look!" Martina said, as she offered the Chihuahua. "A present! His name is Macho. And he's an excellent watch dog."

Serrano didn't want a dog, especially a Chihuahua. But he couldn't say *no*. Not to Martina. The dog *growled* as Serrano took him.

Martina laughed. "Give Macho a treat every now and then. We brought some with us. Isn't that right, Paco?"

The little boy held a bag up for Serrano to see. "Thanks, Paco. Hand me a treat before I get bitten."

Paco opened the bag, chose a bone-shaped biscuit, and passed it over. Macho sniffed the offering, and bit it. Serrano looked at Martina. "Macho isn't the only one who's hungry. I am, too. Can I take you to lunch? I hear that Pancho's is the best restaurant in town."

Martina laughed, and Serrano liked the sound of it. "What you heard is true. Largely because Pancho's is the *only* restaurant in town. But yes, that would be fun. People will talk though."

"Really? What will they say?"

"They'll say that we're having an affair. That's how people are in a small town."

"I can live with that," Serrano replied. Then, before Martina could reply, Serrano took Macho inside.

A faint yapping noise was audible as Serrano left the dog in Emilio's custody and exited the house. "My car?" Serrano inquired.

"Yes, please, my backseat is loaded with groceries," Martina said, as she gestured toward an old Ford Fiesta. It had been red originally. But now, after years under the sun, it was pink.

Pancho's was good. Not great, but good. The tables were organized around a fountain at the center of an internal courtyard, and the service was excellent.

Some of the other diners stared, just as Martina predicted they would. "The news will reach Mexico City by dinner time," she joked.

The conversation was intentionally simple, and free of anything related to violence, until Paco spoke up. He was looking at Serrano as he sucked Coke through a straw. "How many people have you killed?"

"Paco!" Martina exclaimed. "We don't ask questions like that."

"We do if we're eight," Serrano said. "And here's my answer… I don't keep track, because if I did, it would be like a score in a game. It's my hope that I'll never have to kill anyone again. Does that answer your question?"

Paco nodded and his straw made a rattling noise, as he siphoned the last drops of Coke out of his glass. "That was well said," Martina told him. "Thank you."

She looked at her watch. "Paco and I need to get going. We have school tomorrow."

Serrano's eyebrows rose. "We?"

"Yes. I am a maestra. You didn't know?"

"No, I didn't," Serrano replied. "Guerilla, yes. Vocalist, yes. But a teacher? No. I'm impressed."

Martina shrugged. "I'm lucky. I have a way to earn a living. Many people don't. Or, they do, and El Cuchillo steals 3% of their money."

Serrano frowned. "How so?"

"It's a protection racket," Martina replied. "You can be sure that the family who owns this restaurant pays it. Otherwise, there would be a mysterious fire, and Pancho's would burn down. Locals call it 'la roca,' meaning the rock that holds them down." After a moment, Martina added, "Take this place for example. It probably generates something like a 5% profit. So, after the owners pay up, they have 2% of revenues to live on. It's evil."

They left after that and returned to La Casa Bonita, where the pink Fiesta was waiting. The kiss on the cheek was unexpected but welcome. Their eyes met. "Take care, Soldado," Martina said. "This isn't over. It's just beginning." Then she drove away.

Macho was yapping as Serrano entered the house. It lasted five minutes. Then, when the dog finally stopped, he received a treat.

Emilio had left, but a lot of progress had been made, and a new mattress was supposed to arrive the following day.

Serrano opened a beer. The air was hot and the cold liquid felt good going down. There was something he'd been putting off. It had to do with the enigmatic line in Papá's letter: "Protect the weak, and rely on Bruno. He will assist you."

Bruno was a Xoloitzcuintle, or Xolo, one of several breeds of hairless dog. There were three sizes, including standard, intermediate, and miniature. Bruno was a standard Xolo, who had been passionately dedicated to Papá, but didn't care for anyone else, Serrano included.

And, when Bruno died of old age, Papá had a headstone made—and interred the dog next to the house.

So, if Serrano wanted to seek Bruno's help, he'd have to dig the dog up. A chore that shouldn't bother Serrano but did.

The sun was starting to set as Serrano collected the necessary tools, went outside, and began to work. A waist-high adobe wall hid Serrano's macabre task from the neighbors, who were understandably skittish where the Americano was concerned.

The initial task was to remove the pavers that protected the grave and put them aside. Each tile was numbered on the back, which struck Serrano as strange.

Once that task was complete Serrano found himself looking at a dust-covered tarp. Serrano freed the plastic which revealed a coffin below. And there, burned into the wood, were the words, "Here lies Bruno. RIP."

Was that it? A box filled with dog bones? Serrano didn't think so. By kneeling, and reaching down, Serrano was able to grab the lid.

Rather than *creak*, like in a movie, the coffin opened noise-lessly. And there, lying side-by-side were individually sealed packages.

Thanks to his years in the Marine Corps, Serrano could identify them by feel. There were two long guns—sniper rifles probably—and more importantly, three M249 light machine guns!

Though no longer issued by the Marine Corps since the M27 Infantry Automatic Rifle had been introduced, the old Squad Automatic Weapons were battle tested. And Papá knew that.

Properly employed, the SAWs would go a long way toward fighting off the next attack by El Cuchillo's narcos. And the rifles wouldn't hurt either. Serrano planned to grab one for himself. *God Bless you, Papá*, Serrano thought. *And Bruno too.*

It took two days to secretly transfer the weapons and ammo to carefully chosen guerillas. However, the additional guns weren't enough and Serrano knew that. Weapons without training were meaningless.

But, if the guerillas were to train openly, thereby revealing their new weapons, El Cuchillo was bound to learn of it via

Mayor Aguilar or Officer Molina. Both of whom were known to act as spies.

It was Martina who came up with a solution and made the necessary arrangements. Some of the guerillas went on vacation. Others left for a spiritual retreat with Father Colon. And three guerillas left town to participate in a triathlon. Even though they had never participated in such an event before.

Then, twelve hours later, all of them came together on a hacienda managed by a man whose daughter had been kidnapped, and was still missing.

Training began right away. By that time the once amorphous group of fighters had been rebranded as Alpha Company. It was comprised of six squads, each with a leader, and consisting of two, four-person fire teams. Martina was in command and an ex-army noncom named José Herrera was XO. Serrano was listed as an "advisor."

The amount of time spent at the improvised firing line was limited due to the scant supply of ammo. But the brief live-fire exercises did offer the trainees an opportunity to become acquainted with their newly acquired machine guns.

On the second day the company focused on squad level maneuvers, followed by fire team exercises, and learning specific skill sets like communications, first aid, and transportation.

All the while Serrano was walking around shouting, "Shoot! Move! Communicate!

"Don't bunch up. One grenade will kill you all!"

And, "Stay off the skyline damn it!"

The two-day field exercise ended with a carne asada. But even then, Martina insisted on a security perimeter with loaded weapons. "Never assume you are safe. Tu arma es tu amante." *Your gun is your lover.*

It was, Serrano thought, a good beginning.

*

Rancho del Sol, Mexico

Pablo Enrique Ramirez was inside, sitting in his favorite easy chair, as he looked at the pasture where his horses were grazing. It would be nice to ride one.

But, due to the guerra eterna he couldn't. Not without running the risk that a sniper would shoot him.

It was, Ramirez thought, similar to the Late Middle Ages. During that time, European principalities ruled by princes and dukes waged endless war on each other.

And that, Ramirez believed, was analogous to the battles between Mexico's drug lords. The list was long, and included Los Tecnos, Las Patriotas, Los Ceros, his cartel Los Ortegos, Los Caribes, and last but not least, Las Rojas. A cartel led by Elena Isabella Ayo. A handsome woman with reddish hair. Thus, the cartel's name.

All of Ramirez's competitors were dangerous. But Las Rojas were of the greatest concern, because their territory bordered his to the south, and Ayo wanted to expand.

A chime sounded and Ramierz's major domo appeared. His name was Balasco. "Officer Molina is here, sir."

Ramirez sighed. Lugar de Paz. The town was a thorn in his side. As was the need to deal with an idiota like Officer Molina.

Ramirez stood and turned to face his visitor. "Officer Molina! It's a pleasure to see you!"

Molina knew the greeting for what it was: mierda. The man standing before him was tall, at least six-two and armed with a sheath knife. Was it the one used to carve the letter "C" into Molina's chest? The blade was sheathed so the policeman couldn't tell.

"Gracias," Molina responded, as he battled the desire to pee. "It's good to see you as well."

"Please," Ramirez said, gesturing to an overstuffed chair. "I'm going to light a cigar. Would you care to join me?"

Molina was afraid to say *no*, so he said, "Sí. Gracias."

"Balasco!" Ramirez exclaimed, as he sat down. "Bring cigars. The ones from Cuba, por favor."

Balasco arrived with an open humidor and the special lighter Ramirez insisted on. Molina watched the drug lord rotate his cigar over the flame, without letting it touch, before taking a puff.

So, when Balasco offered the humidor to Molina, he copied Ramirez and couldn't help but cough.

Ramirez smiled indulgently. "Tell me, Jorge, how's it going in the charming village of Lugar de Paz?"

"That's why I came," Molina said, as he held the cigar well away from his face. "A man came to town. Three Mexicans tried to kill him. They're dead.

"Then *four* Americanos broke into his home. He killed them too. The townspeople call him 'El Soldado.'"

"Please use the ashtray next to your chair," Ramirez said, as some ash landed on the wood floor. "The soldier... Was he one?"

Molina nodded eagerly. "A United States Marine. And he spends a lot of time with Martina Blanco."

The drug lord's eyebrows rose. "Are they lovers?"

Molina shrugged. "I don't know. What I *do* know is that Blanco plans to visit Guadalupe and take part in the upcoming Day of the Dead celebration. Blanco is going to perform there. She's a singer."

Ramirez frowned. "How do you know this?"

"There are posters all over town," Molina replied. "Some

townspeople would go to the festival regardless. But Blanco's performance is another reason to go."

"And Mayor Aguilar?" Ramirez inquired. "How's he? Well, I hope."

Molina was paid to keep an eye on Aguilar, who in turn, was paid to watch him. "The mayor is fine. And, if I'm not mistaken, he shares my concerns regarding the mestizo."

"Which are?"

"That he could lead a revolt."

Ramirez stubbed his cigar out, which allowed Molina to do likewise. "Balasco! The box!"

When the major domo appeared, he was carrying a beautifully crafted wooden box, which he presented to Ramirez.

After flipping the lid back, Ramirez selected a gold peso. Although the coin's face value was only twenty pesos, its intrinsic melt value was $977.82 on that particular day.

Ramirez said, "Catch!" and tossed the coin. Molina fumbled the catch, and was forced to get up and go after the gold disk.

Ramirez laughed.

Lugar de Paz, Mexico

Barber Herman Burgos had been crippled by a car accident. "But you can fight the narcos from your rooftop," Martina assured him. "By warning us when they're on the way."

And it was true. By learning to fly the commercial drones donated by Nick Serrano, Burgos and a rotating team of other pilots could monitor the approaches to town and provide two minutes of warning before El Cuchillo's men entered the community.

It wasn't much, but some warning was better than none, especially at night. And Burgos was proud of his contribution.

The barber was sitting on his roof, wrapped in a blanket,

when the first headlights appeared. Then, as more lights populated the screen, Burgos felt a rising sense of excitement.

His phone was on and ready. The first 25 messages went out to leadership and specialists. The second group of texts alerted the rest of Alpha Company. Lights came on in houses all over Lugar de Paz.

Serrano awoke to the sound of his phone going off, swore, and hurried to dress. The rig went on last. Then, rifle in hand, he hurried downhill toward Kill Box One.

The plan was to capture the incoming vehicles in one of three intersections, where expendable cars would be used to box the narcos in, even as automatic fire poured down on the invaders from the surrounding rooftops. A plan which, Serrano hoped, would maximize enemy casualties, and minimize the danger posed by friendly fire.

Serrano arrived just as an old car braked, and slid sideways to block the street. The driver jumped out, and ran as a SAW opened fire.

"Three-round bursts." That's what the gunners had been taught. And the incoming vehicles were hard to miss. Slugs peppered enemy vehicles, killing some narcos before they could get out, even as snipers fired on those who were lucky enough to exit their vehicles.

Serrano was standing half-hidden by the corner of a building, firing on the "runners," when Molotov cocktails began to rain down on the motionless autos.

Flames spread, found gas tanks, and triggered explosions. It was the one-sided slaughter that Serrano had envisioned.

Or, it would have been, except for one thing: Half of the narcos were on horseback! And arrived in trucks which delivered them to the edge of town.

Serrano heard the clatter of hooves from behind him, and

was in the process of turning, when a horse shouldered him aside. The animal's rider uttered a whoop of joy.

The rifle went flying and Serrano fell. He was lying on his back as the narco pulled his horse around and charged.

Shorty seemed to jump into Serrano's hand and fire on its own. The recoil jolted Serrano's arm, and the noise assaulted his ears as the .357 hollow points hit the horse in the chest.

The animal staggered and was in the process of going down when its rider jumped free. And, in an impressive example of horsemanship, landed on his feet.

The narco was a 9mm aficionado and was taking aim when Serrano fired, and continued to fire. A man makes a lot smaller target than a horse, and the distance was well beyond the short-barreled pistol's normal reach. *Accurate* reach anyway, which was why Serrano unloaded on the asshole.

And the shotgun approach worked. The narco toppled over backwards, as Serrano stood and drew the long gun. A car alarm was bleating, a horse was screaming, and the bang bang bang of an assault weapon could be heard over both.

A narco limped toward Serrano, hurrying to reload, but not in time. The S&W spoke, and a .357 magnum slug blew half of the man's face away, leaving his body to spin and fall.

A column of invaders appeared out of the drifting smoke and Serrano shot them, one after the other, until the last man tried to turn away. Serrano killed him.

It was second nature to release the cylinder, shake the empties out, and drop a moon clip into place. Serrano was about to flip the weapon closed when someone jumped onto his back.

He threw himself back, landed on top of his assailant, and rolled off. That was when Serrano realized that his attacker was a young woman.. Their eyes locked. Serrano flipped the cylinder closed. "Don't do it."

The woman lunged at Serrano, knife raised, and was about to stab him when a bullet slammed into her head.

Martina appeared out of the haze, pistol in hand, one sleeve wet with blood. She offered her free hand and Serrano took it. She pulled him up. He acknowledged with a "Thanks."

"De nada," Martina replied. "You're the one who deserves gratitude."

Serrano shook his head. "I didn't consider the possibility of horses."

"That will keep you humble," Martina answered. "Come on... We have work to do."

And that was true. There were wounded to take care of, weapons to collect, and ammo to harvest.

Last, but not least, there were bodies to bury. Enough dead to keep coffin maker Jorge Gómez, undertaker Tomás Pérez, and Father Colon busy for days.

Slowly, as if reluctant to shine on Mexico, the sun began to rise.

Chapter Five

Southbound toward San Luis Potosí, Mexico

Nearly a week had passed since the attack on Lugar de Paz. The Federales had come and gone. And why not? Local citizens had the right to bear arms, and to defend themselves against "parties unknown." Although everyone knew that El Cuchillo was behind the assault.

So, peace had been restored to the Place of Peace. That left Serrano and Martina free to travel to Guadalupe, where she was scheduled to perform.

The ostensible reason for Serrano's presence was to serve as Martina's one-man security detail. But there was a secondary agenda as well, and that was to have some time by themselves. Both felt something for the other. But what was it? Perhaps a road trip would provide an answer.

Nuestra Señora de la Santa Muerte, often shortened to Santa Muerte, was a Mexican folk saint. Strangely, to Serrano's way of thinking, even though Santa Muerte was said to be "Our Lady of Holy Death," she was associated with healing, protection, and a safe delivery to the afterlife.

In recent times, the number of participants in a day of celebration of the saint's life had grown to over 12 million. Because of that, November second, the Day of the Dead, was big business. Taken together, travel, hospitality, costumes, and the endless tchotchkes associated with the celebration generated millions in revenue.

And Martina was part of that. A performance in Guadalupe would generate the extra cash needed to save for Paco's education, and for a new used car.

They were driving Serrano's Taurus. The countryside was hilly, dry, and given to patches of green. The occasional cell tower was visible in the distance. But, other than that, there was very little to see except for a few isolated houses—and an occasional cow.

"So, what will you do when the fighting stops?" Martina inquired.

Serrano glanced at her. "It's going to stop?"

"We can hope, can't we?"

"No," Serrano said. "I don't think we can. But maybe, just maybe, we can create an island to live on. A place of peace. Lugar de Paz."

"Such an island would have to be strong," Martina replied. "Too strong for strong men to attack."

"Exactly," Serrano responded. "So, to answer your question, I hope to create an island of peace within the larger peace and build a new life."

"What about the old life?"

"Valerie stole my life savings and I detest her."

"I'm sorry," Martina said. "So, you don't have any children?"

"No. Valerie said kids would be a lot of work, and might ruin her figure. She wants to be a social media influencer."

Martina laughed. "You *are* a hard luck case. Fortunately, not all women are like Valerie."

"No, they aren't," Serrano agreed as he looked at her. "Some are very different."

"Keep your eyes on the road," Martina said primly.

Serrano did as he was told. Were things going well? Yes, he thought they were.

The distance between San Luis Potosí and Guadalupe was 245 miles, and rather than push through, the couple agreed to stay the night in San Luis Potosí and complete their journey the following day. The medium-priced hotel chosen was located on the edge of the business district, and surrounded by other well-kept multistory buildings.

Because San Luis Potosí was a state capital, Federales were everywhere, causing Serrano to ask why the city had what seemed like a thousand policemen, while Lugar de Paz had only one. Assuming Molina qualified as a law enforcement officer.

"Because," Martina replied. "The politicians want to be safe."

Serrano knew she was correct.

After parking the car, the pair entered the hotel's lobby, and waited to check in. Serrano had his AWOL bag. She had a suitcase.

Serrano requested separate rooms on the same floor, and wound up with cross-hall mini suites. With that accomplished they went upstairs to park their luggage prior to dinner.

It turned out that the term "mini-suite" stemmed from the fact that each room had a couch and a chair. Not that it mattered.

They chose the restaurant across the street. It was filled with "suits." Men mostly, who were talking about money, sex, or power—and how to obtain more of each.

Serrano and Martina's conversation was quite different. Paco was being bullied, her car was dying a slow death, and the school's principal was taking heat for Martina's role as a part-time guerilla.

"So," Martina said, as their desserts arrived. "Enough about me. I know you want to protect Lugar de Paz. But surely you have other interests as well."

There was a long pause while Serrano tried to think of one. He couldn't. "I joined the Marine Corps at 18. And I was a mercenary after that. That's all I am. Or am likely to be."

Martina placed a hand on top of his. "Protecting the weak is the highest calling there is," she assured him. And, judging from the look in Martina's eyes, she meant it. Serrano felt a sense of gratitude.

After dinner they went upstairs to their rooms. Martina kissed Serrano's cheek and said, "Sweet dreams," before turning to unlock her door.

Serrano waited until Martina was safely inside before entering his room. Then he made the usual nest on the floor, brushed his teeth, and flopped on the bed. *I'll teach Paco how to fight.* That's what Serrano was thinking when he heard a soft knock.

Pistol in hand, Serrano put an eye to the peephole, and saw Martina. He opened the door and she entered. He then closed the door and secured it. "What's up?"

Martina's eyes were big and brown. They locked with his. "I was lonely. Like I've been for a long time. But not now."

Serrano took Martina into his arms. They kissed the kind of kiss that's a promise of things to come, and gradually made their way to the bed. "Where are the pillows?" Martina inquired.

Serrano shrugged. "I sleep on the floor."

Serrano feared that Martina would think he was crazy. She nodded soberly. "So do I." Both of them laughed.

"But not tonight," Martina said, as she began to remove her clothes.

Serrano hurried to get the pillows and put them on the bed. He was about to strip when Martina stepped in to undo Serrano's belt buckle. "I'll take care of that," she said. "And everything else that needs to be taken care of. But watch my arm. It hasn't healed yet."

Once naked, they lay on the bed. Martina's black hair was fanned out under her head, her nipples were hard, and her legs were slightly parted. "I'm yours, Soldado... But remember, it's been a long time for me. So be gentle."

Serrano was gentle. And the lovemaking took a long time, followed by a second passion-fueled session, which ended quickly.

And then Martina began to cry. Her chest heaved as the sobs came, one after another, and tears rolled down her cheeks. "What's wrong?" an anxious Serrano wanted to know, as he used a sheet to blot her face. "Did I hurt you?"

"N-n-no," Martina replied. "Nothing's wrong. I'm crying because everything is right."

Serrano held her close. And then, after some snuggling, he spoke. "So, are you going to confess to Father Colon?"

Martina laughed, and giggled. "Not in a hundred years."

They slept after that. And, when Serrano awoke, Martina was gone.

Serrano showered, shaved, and got dressed. He then put the rig on and checked his weapons before donning the jacket. Martina knocked shortly thereafter, and they had breakfast in the hotel's restaurant.

The relationship felt different. They shared a bench seat rather than sit opposite from each other. There was some touching under the table. And the conversation was light hearted.

Serrano relished the intimacy of it. A feeling he'd never experienced with Valerie. And never missed because he didn't know it was possible.

After finishing their meal, they checked out. It was November second, the day of the Santa Muerte Festival, and Martina was scheduled for a rehearsal at five. So, it was important to get going.

Martina's performance was at the behest of the Catholic Church, which continually blasted the Santa Muerte cult as blasphemous and satanic. More than that, the Pope called the Santa Muerte movement an "extension of narco culture."

So, rather than allow the festival to go unanswered, the church was offering two hours of counter programming—set to begin with a performance by the woman billed as "Angel Face." Which was to say Martina Blanco, dressed as an angel, and singing *Blest Be the Lord*.

That's why it was important to get an early start, push the top of the speed limit, and keep the bio breaks short. They took turns driving, ate a fast-food lunch, and were back on the road in less than an hour.

Guadalupe was part of the greater Monterrey metropolitan area. And that meant heavy traffic during rush hour. But even though the flow was slow, it was steady, and they managed to arrive at the hotel in time to grab a bite.

Then it was time for Martina to head for her rehearsal, leaving Serrano to sample the festival, before attending the performance. "Here," Serrano said, as he offered the derringer. "Stash it somewhere."

Martina was reluctant at first, but eventually tucked the gun away. "I'm not used to having someone protect me," she said. "But I like it. Give me a kiss."

Their lips met. And, when the kiss threatened to turn into something more, she pushed him away. "Angels don't kiss! Not until later. I'll see you later. After the performance."

Serrano waved as a cab took her away. Darkness had descended on the city, and the Santa Muerte celebration was in full swing, as Serrano entered the crowd. A street had been blocked off, and it was packed with revelers. The air was heavy with the mixed odors of marijuana, incense and street food. And the crowd was a heady mix of tourists, street vendors, drogadictos, policemen, pickpockets, and families—some trailing small children who struggled to keep up.

People dressed as hollow-eyed calaveras drank beer and "bumped" tourists, while their fingers probed for valuables. Whores, some dressed in wedding gowns, plied their trade. And circuladores peddled their wares.

Serrano stared as a skeleton on stilts teetered through the crowd, and a ghoul wearing a top hat walked arm in arm with his dead bride—who was clutching a bouquet of black flowers.

According to Martina, what all the celebrants had in common was a belief in, and a devotion to, Santa Muerte. An unsaintly saint willing to drink, have sex, and protect those who were plagued by poverty, lawless cops, and crooked politicians.

An engine growled, and the crowd parted as a truck pulled a float carrying a living likeness of the saint through the throng. Her mask resembled a fleshless skull. And a cowl, heavy with medallions, framed her face.

The saint's top consisted of two cups connected by a chain. Her midriff was bare, and a gauzy skirt flowed from shapely hips, partially revealing slender legs.

The final touch was the gold cross that dangled from her neck. One of the many symbols believers had "borrowed" from the church.

Costumed children rode the float as well, and showered the crowd with bits of black licorice, as a niño thumped a drum.

And that was the moment when a street urchin emerged from the crowd to push a flyer at Serrano. "Ella vale dinero, señor. Estar atento."

The words were enough to trigger Serrano's curiosity. He eyed the poster. And much to his horror, discovered that he was looking at Martina!

At the bottom of the page, it said: "Ayúdanos a encontrar a nuestra madre." Followed by: "$100 U.S." and a phone number. That was a lot of money here.

What felt like ice water trickled into Serrano's veins. Had El Cuchillo's men produced the flyer? Of course they had. And, if someone delivered Martina into their hands, the narcos would kill her.

Should he call the number? Pretend to have her, and meet with them?

No. The narcos would insist on a video of her.

Did they know about her performance? No. Serrano didn't think so. Why produce the flyer if they did?

On the other hand, they knew Martina was at the festival. And all it would take was a stage hand, a makeup artist, or a musician to give her away. Serrano began to run. He had to reach the basilica before the narcos did.

The Basilica of Our Lady of Guadalupe was located at the foot of a hill, roughly half a mile away. It was well lit, and Serrano caught glimpses of the dome as he forced his way through the crowd.

The rehearsal was about to begin. Martina was standing to one side, well clear of the Basilica's altar, across from the formally attired musicians. The local bishop was about to introduce her when shouts were heard from the back of the nave, and two files of demons entered in, one from each side—waving assault rifles. "¡Abajo! ¡Abajo! ¡Abajo!" a ghoul shouted, as he fired his weapon into the air. The performers screamed and ducked, covering their heads with their hands.

The bullets shattered one of the high-arched windows above, causing broken glass to fall on the musicians. One went down with a serious head wound.

The living dead were forced to hesitate, as a brave policeman entered the nave, and fired at a ghoul.

Bursts of 5.56x45mm rounds cut the lawman down. "The Angel! Get her!" a linen-swathed corpse yelled. And Martina knew the creature meant her.

A skeletal demon rushed at Martina. A hollow point bullet from Serrano's derringer punctured his throat. Blood sprayed as the body collapsed into a pool of gore. Then the living corpse issued new orders. "¡Mátala!"

Martina took a dive, and elbowed her way through the pool of blood, to gain the scant protection offered by a pew.

Serrano heard the gunshots while racing up the steps to the Basilica. He pulled both pistols, firing both at once.

Those who could flee had already done so by the time Serrano entered the nave. He could see the dead cop, the scattering of glass, and a broken angel wing up front.

Rage surged through Serrano's body. There were two groups of tangos, and Serrano fired at both targets as he made his way up the center aisle.

A demon was thrown forward as a bullet hit him in the back. Another turned to confront the menace when a .358 round punched a hole through his chest. He fell backwards.

A ghoul threw his weapon down and raised his hands. Serrano shot him, and threw himself sideways, as a blast of automatic fire tore into the spot where he'd been.

Then help came from on high as a much-bloodied angel rose

from her hiding place to fire a captured assault weapon. She killed two of them before the rest fled.

Serrano went forward to embrace Martina, and was whispering "Gracias a Dios" over and over again, as Federales flooded the nave, beat Serrano to the floor and hauled him away.

Chapter Six

Lugar de Paz, Mexico

Two days had passed since the attack in the Basilica. Serrano was still sore from the beating he'd taken, followed by a night spent in jail. A nasty place packed with lawbreakers who were still made-up to resemble ghouls and demons.

But thanks to Martina, along with the efforts of the priests who'd been present during the attack, and those of the local bishop, Serrano had been released at 10:15 in the morning.

The police chief thanked him. The bishop thanked him. And Martina thanked him with a kiss. And that was reward enough.

The diocese paid Martina in spite of the canceled performance, and promised to bring her back at Christmas, which wasn't that far away.

The drive home was boring, except for the night in San Luis Potosí, which was very enjoyable indeed—even if some pain accompanied the pleasure.

Now, back in Lugar de Paz, it was time to take out the trash. Meaning Officer Molina.

Serrano couldn't prove that Molina had leaked Martina's travel plans to El Cuchillo, but all the townspeople agreed that he was a spy, and that was good enough.

After feeding Macho, and buckling the rig into place, Serrano went out to the Taurus. The word *lávame* had been inscribed in the thick layer of dust that covered the car, and Serrano added *wash car* to his list of things to do.

Molina lived in a one-room adobe dwelling just north of town. Serrano arrived shortly after nine to find that the policeman's car was still there, parked next to an ancient pickup. Serrano wasn't surprised. All the townspeople knew that Molina didn't roll out until ten or so.

Serrano saw no reason to be subtle. So, he drew the long gun and kicked the flimsy door open. It banged against a wall. As Serrano entered, Molina was reaching for the shotgun resting next to his rumpled bed. "Don't do it," Serrano advised.

Molina let his hand drop and opened his mouth to speak.

"Shut up," Serrano said, as he sat on a wooden chair. "Here's the deal. I know you told El Cuchillo about Martina Blanco's performance in Guadalupe. But I can't prove it." He considered Molina for a moment. "So, rather than shoot you in the face, I'm going to send you out to pollute some other town. Hand me your phone."

Molina had to pat the bedding in order to find the phone, which he gave to Serrano. "Now," Serrano said. "Jot down the password for the phone, and the laptop that's sitting next to the sink. I'll test both while you load your stuff into the pickup. And, if you have some blood money stashed somewhere, keep it. I sure as hell don't want it."

It took Molina the better part of an hour to load his belongings into the truck. Serrano was there to see him off. "The way I see it, you have two choices: Run to El Cuchillo and ask him to hire you, or look for another town to infect. I suggest option two, because you no longer have anything to offer El Cuchillo. And he's likely to use you for target practice. But hey, that's just me. It's up to you. Vaya con Dios."

Then, Serrano shot time-stamped video of Molina entering his truck and driving away.

With that accomplished, Serrano drove to Mayor Aguilar's office. Various citizens were waiting to get help. And Aguilar's secretary tried to stop Serrano from entering the office but failed.

An elderly lady was seated in the mayor's guest chair and Serrano removed his hat. "Disculpe, señora. Tengo algo urgente que decirle al alcalde."

Then, turning to Aguilar, Serrano said, "Officer Molina asked me to pass along the following message: Rather than continue to work for the citizens of Lugar de Paz, he's going to seek employment elsewhere, and wanted you to have this."

Serrano tossed the star-shaped badge onto the desk, turned to the woman and nodded. "Gracias, señora." Then he left.

Paco had just returned from school when Serrano arrived at the Blanco residence. He already had his mother's permission to accompany Señor Serrano on "a special outing."

The old gravel pit was south of town, and the spot where the town's gun owners went to bust caps and have some cervezas.

As Serrano got out of the car, hundreds of empty shell casings twinkled in the afternoon sun. Serrano didn't approve. *Always police your brass.* That's what Papá said. And Serrano's Marine Corps instructors agreed.

Gravel crunched as Serrano went to the back of the car, opened the trunk, and removed a package. It was wrapped in camo patterned paper and tied with string.

Paco was waiting nearby and Serrano gave him the box. "This is for you, son. Your mother said it would be okay."

The boy was no fool. So, given the location, plus the size of the package, Paco had a pretty good idea of what was waiting inside. And, after ripping the paper off and opening the box,

Paco saw what he hoped to see—a pistol.

"Go ahead, take it out," Serrano said. "Never point it at someone or something you don't plan to shoot. Especially me."

Paco took the weapon out and pointed it at the rusty gravel chute a hundred feet away. "What you're holding is an Old West style, nine shot, .22 revolver with a swing-out cylinder," Serrano said. "Happy birthday."

Paco looked at Serrano. "I was born in May."

"That's right," Serrano agreed. "But I couldn't make the party." Serrano patted Paco on the shoulder. "Alright. It's time to memorize all the parts. There will be a test. And, if you score high enough, you'll get to fire twenty-seven rounds."

The next forty-five minutes were spent naming the different parts of the revolver, as Paco cocked the hammer, eased it down, released the cylinder, swung it out, and pretended to insert bullets.

The weapon was used, but in excellent condition. And, like most guns in Mexico, it had been purchased on the black market. That was because there were only two legal gun stores in Mexico. The Directorate for the Commercialization of Arms and Munitions located near the capital, and a second outlet in Apodaca, Nuevo León.

That forced people who wanted to buy legally to potentially travel long distances and wait for months after completing a stack of paperwork.

Background checks made sense in Serrano's opinion. But the DCAM process was stupid. Especially in a country where it was so much easier to buy a smuggled weapon.

The live fire exercise went well because Serrano did what Papá did, which was let Paco fire at empty Coke cans from twelve feet away. After scoring seven hits, the boy felt like a million pesos and the first class came to an end.

Paco babbled like a magpie all the way home, about shooting, yes, but about other things as well. Serrano listened the way Papá always listened to him.

Finally, when Serrano returned to La Casa Bonita, it was to find that two cop cars were sitting out front. And four Federales were there to greet him. One was a sergeant. Serrano held his hands up, palms out. "Don't tell me, let me guess. Mayor Aguilar sent you."

"Yes," the sergeant replied. "He says you murdered Officer Molina."

"Except that I didn't," Serrano replied. "And I'll prove it. But I need to open the trunk of my car. You can stand next to me while I do it."

"Place your weapons on the ground," the sergeant ordered. "Then you can open the trunk."

Serrano drew each weapon, using two fingers only, and laid them on the ground. Then, with the sergeant at his side, he opened the trunk.

"That's Officer Molina's laptop," Serrano said. "And that's his phone. Both devices contain emails in which Molina conspired with El Cuchillo to attack Lugar de Paz.

"Except it didn't work. Martina Blanco and her guerillas defeated El Cuchillo's men.

"So," Serrano said loudly, as he turned to face the rest of them. "You have everything you need to arrest ex-officer Molina and Señor Ramirez.

"By the way, I taped Molina getting into his truck and leaving. Hopefully for good. The video is time stamped."

Of course, he could have murdered Molina *after* he left Luga de Paz. But, with no body, there was no case.

Serrano watched the Federales exchange glances. They knew that some of their superiors were on the take. And they knew that trying to arrest Ramirez would be a suicide mission.

"Gracias," the sergeant said, as he took charge of the electronics. "We will investigate and let you know if we need more information."

"That sounds good," Serrano replied. "And oh, by the way, I have copies of the relevant emails. So, should the messages on those devices go astray somehow, I can provide backups."

Serrano smiled broadly. No one smiled back. The Federales knew a threat when they heard one.

Serrano watched the policemen get into their cars and drive away. Case closed.

Life settled into a comfortable routine after that. Maintenance projects during the day, a session with Paco after school, and some quality time with Martina in the evening.

Then Father Colon came to see him, and everything changed.

Macho started yapping a full thirty seconds before Serrano heard the knock on the door. Serrano answered the way he always did, pistol at the ready. "Who is it?"

"Father Colon."

Serrano peered through the peephole to confirm that the clergy man was alone. He opened the door. "Seven PM? What's up?"

"I need help," Colon replied. "*Your* help."

"Okay," Serrano said, as Macho nosed the priest. "Have a seat."

The cleric was clearly distraught, judging from the expression on his face, and the way he was fidgeting. "I have a confession to make."

"That's supposed to work the other way around," Serrano replied.

"Give me your crucifix. The one hanging on the wall."

The cross had been placed there by Papá. Serrano had seen

no need to remove it. He got up, went over, and took the crucifix down. Colon extended his hand. It was shaking.

Then, with the cross clutched in both hands, Colon went to his knees. And, when he spoke, it was clearly to God rather than Serrano.

"Forgive me, Father, for I have sinned. I am not asking for absolution, because I cannot absolve myself, and I don't deserve your grace. There was a time, shortly after I graduated from seminary, that I fell in love with a congregant. And she with me. Part of that attraction was physical. An urge so strong that I couldn't, and didn't, resist. That in spite of my oath of celibacy. As a result, a life was created which could not be extinguished without committing an even greater sin. A baby was born. A beautiful girl baby, who was raised by her mother, with financial assistance from me. Eventually, roughly a year ago, this beautiful spirit fell into bad company—and became part of a godless group led by an evil man. And now, even though she wants to leave, she can't. Her name is Pia. And I must free Pia if I can. I'm not asking for your blessing, which I don't deserve, but I beg you to intercede for her. Amen."

As Colon looked up tears were streaming down his cheeks. Their eyes met. "You are my hope," Colon said. "My only hope. I fear there will be fighting."

Serrano stood and offered his hand. "Get up, Father. We have work to do."

It took more than an hour to prepare for the 507-mile journey. Then Serrano made calls to Emilio and Martina, informing them of the trip. But not the reason for it, since that was a private matter. Emilio promised to feed Macho, and keep an eye on the house.

A two-lane road led to an autopista that would take them

south to Mexico City. Serrano drove while the priest shared what he'd been able to learn from Pia's mother and the internet. The Acara Foundation was dedicated to "The Second Way," meaning a more spiritual way of life. And, rather than a conventional building, the Foundation was housed in an imitation Aztec pyramid.

"The organization is funded by 'life tithes,'" Colon added. "Those who want to join, and thousands have, must donate one tenth of their net worth to the organization. And then, after being accepted, they're required to surrender one tenth of their monthly income.

"Their leader, a man named Sabastian Acara, is a body builder and ex-male model, who enjoys Mexico City's nightlife.

"More than that, Acara claims to channel the Aztec god Patecatl, who is the god of healing and fertility.

"And according to historical records, Patecatl claimed to have discovered peyote, which his adherents use during their secret rites. That includes sex orgies—if the rumors are true. Which would help explain why people pay large sums of money to belong."

"Why doesn't the government crack down on them?" Serrano inquired. "Peyote is illegal."

"Generally speaking, it is," Colon agreed. "But peyote *is* allowed for religious purposes. And that's what the Foundation is, according to Acara. A religion."

"So, Pia is a member?"

"Yes," Colon replied. "And according to Camila, her mother, she's a prisoner."

"How does Camila know that?"

"Camila found an anonymous letter in her mailbox from someone who identified themselves as 'Pia's friend.'

"And, as reported by the friend, Pia is no longer allowed to come and go freely, and is being held in SL1. Whatever that means."

Serrano had questions. Lots of them. But decided to put them on hold for the moment. He could tell that Colon was distraught and there would be plenty of time to chat during the trip.

They took turns driving, stopped for gas when necessary, and stayed the night in a midlevel hotel. Serrano took the opportunity to do some online research. The password for Papá's laptop was written on the machine. A sure sign that no secrets waited within.

It took fifteen minutes of trial and error to find the blueprints for The Azteca, the name by which the Acara step pyramid was known. In accordance with the law, the plans had been filed with the city of San Antonio Tecomitl, where The Azteca was located.

The next two hours were spent poring over the blueprints floor by floor, searching for locations where Pia might be held. There were lots of possibilities.

"That's a lot of territory to cover," Father Colon said, as he looked over Serrano's shoulder.

"It is," Serrano agreed. "Especially with a lot of people around. But look at this."

The site had been bookmarked, and, as Serrano clicked it open, the priest found himself looking at the Foundation's home page.

Serrano chose a heading labeled "Events," and clicked on it. As Serrano scrolled down, he noticed that almost every day featured an event of some sort. They had titles like: "Exploring the Space Within," "Pilates and Patecatl," and "Dreamscapes."

The one day that wasn't given over to some sort of programming was Wednesday, which was labeled "Closed."

"Today's Monday," Serrano said. "We'll go in day after tomorrow. And, if things get iffy, there will be fewer bystanders to worry about."

They rose early the next day, ate breakfast at Starbucks, and were on the road by seven. Traffic was light at first and they made good time. But, as they neared Mexico City, everything shifted to a crawl, and that was despite Serrano's effort to circle around the famously congested metroplex.

At one point it was necessary to venture off the freeway, where they purchased gas, items from a novelty store, and some tacos. Then it was time to resume the trip.

Colon was uncommunicative, and Serrano knew why. For all the priest knew, his daughter was in great danger.

By the time they arrived in San Antonio Tecomitl, it was too late to do anything other than check into a hotel and get some sleep, prior to what Serrano referred to as "D-Day minus one."

Serrano was about to hit the sack when his phone rang. It was Martina. "Where are you?" she wanted to know.

"Mexico City. Or close by."

"Why?" Martina demanded. "If you weren't with a priest, I'd be worried."

"Father Colon sought my advice regarding some personal matters," Serrano replied. "And how could I refuse?"

"By saying 'no,'" Martina answered. "Perhaps you noticed that I am a woman."

"It came to my attention."

"Good. Women know things. They *feel* things. And I'm no exception. I sense danger. Be careful. I want you back. And Paco wants you back."

"What about Macho?"

"He wants dog treats. It doesn't matter who provides them."

Serrano laughed. The conversation ended. Dreams followed.

None of them were good.

Serrano awoke feeling tired, met Father Colon in the hotel's restaurant, and ordered coffee before anything else. By prior agreement Colon was wearing street garb, rather than priestly attire, which would have made him more memorable.

They spoke in low tones. "We need to reconnoiter," Serrano said. "And there's bound to be cameras, which may or may not photograph our plates. We'll need to rent a vehicle under an assumed name. I can pay cash. But the rental agency will ask for ID."

Colon frowned and took a sip of tea. "Here's an idea… I'll wear my black cassock and white collar. And, when they ask for ID, I'll tell them I lost it."

"A lie?" Serrano inquired.

"Yes," Colon admitted. "But for a good purpose."

Serrano grinned. "I like the way you think."

The waitress took their orders, and gave Serrano a refill. Then she left.

"So," Serrano began. "Let's assume the rental scam works. The next step is a slow drive around the pyramid during which you'll shoot a video so we can figure out where we can park and climb onto the The Azteca's lowest roof. Maybe there's a maintenance door there roof – we'll need a big-ass crow bar. And we also need to figure out what 'closed on Wednesdays' actually means."

By the time they left the restaurant the men had a rough plan. *Which will guide us until it doesn't* was the way Serrano put it.

The first step went off without a hitch. Thanks to Colon's attire, and priestly manner—plus a fistful of cash—he was able to rent a white van and drive it away.

Theoretically, since the van was taller than a car, it would make it that much easier to climb onto the pyramid's lowest roof level. And, during a quick stop at a hardware store, the men were able to secure a large pry bar, along with other items that might come in handy.

Then, with Colon's phone at the ready, they circled the step pyramid. Hopefully, luck would be with them, and the men would find a good place to park and climb.

Unfortunately, Serrano didn't see such a spot during the drive-around, but was determined to reserve judgment until they reviewed the video later in a supermarket parking lot.

The first couple of minutes left Serrano feeling hopeless. There weren't any spots where the van could get in close to the building and look natural.

But then, as the entrance to the parking garage appeared, Serrano perked up. "Stop the video... This looks promising."

"*Really?*" Colon asked skeptically. "I see two guards."

"As do I," Serrano replied. "But they can be neutralized. The real question has to do with hours. Will the garage be open tomorrow? Even though the rest of the place is locked down? Inquiring minds want to know."

The video had been transferred to Papá's laptop via email. The priest lowered his head in order to see better. "There's a sign. It reads, 'Garage open for deliveries 7 days a week, 9-5.'"

"Damn!" Serrano exclaimed. "That's wonderful!"

"Swearing is a sin," Colon said.

Serrano started to reply. Started to remind Colon of *his* sins. But thought better of it. What did Jesus say? Something about casting stones. So, he turned his thoughts to the challenge ahead. And now, with thanks to the latest intel, Serrano knew what to do.

Chapter Seven

San Antonio Tecomitl, Mexico

It was Wednesday morning, and Pedro Riviera was bored. The Foundation was closed but vendors could still make deliveries. However, since the guards couldn't sign for shipments, only a few vendors chose to do so.

Pedro and his buddy Alfonso took note as a white van slowed, signaled, and turned. Pedro was surprised to see that the driver and his passenger were wearing sombreros. What the fuck?

Then, as the van came to a halt, Pedro realized that the driver was wearing a Day of the Dead calavera mask. "Is this the Ambassador hotel?" the driver inquired.

"No, idiotas," Pedro replied. "That's one block to the east."

Serrano shot the guard with his Taser X2, shifted his aim, and nailed the second man as well. Both men spasmed, tried to stay vertical, but failed.

Serrano turned to Colon. "They're down. Go for it."

The priest got out and tires screeched as Serrano hit the gas. The plan called for him to turn the van around while Colon used zip ties to secure the guards.

Once the van was positioned for a quick getaway, Serrano hurried over to the guard kiosk. The gate controls consisted of two buttons: Arriba and Abajo.

The down button was red, and Serrano thumbed it.

The see-through barrier clattered as it came down, and barred all vehicles from entering or leaving.

The guards were swearing, kicking and rolling around by then. Father Colon stuffed a handkerchief into each mouth and secured them with tape.

The skull mask was scratchy, and the plastic vaquero costume was hot, but Serrano wasn't about to remove either with the many cameras around, mounted on the ceiling. Were they being monitored somewhere? If so, the intruders would have company soon.

Serrano took a look around. *SL1.* That's where Pia was being held. Or *had* been held. There was no way to know. But even Father Colon agreed that they couldn't search the entire pyramid. So, it was SL1 or nothing.

A large floor-by-floor wall chart was available for the guards to refer to as shipments arrived. And sure enough, SL1 equated to *Sub-Level 1.*

"I see an elevator," Colon announced. "Let's go."

Lattice work doors parted to reveal a no-frills freight elevator plastered with safety signs. Serrano noticed that in addition to SL1, there was a SL2, and a SL3. Both of which were dedicated to parking.

The elevator jerked, whirred, and descended. The doors parted to reveal signs including, HVAC, Power, and Water next to an arrow pointed to the right. Storage was to the left. And Pia was being "stored." Kind of.

"We'll go left," Serrano announced. "Bring that shotgun around. Chances are that you'll need it."

The sawed-off shotgun was Serrano's, and the only weapon Colon might be able to use successfully, since he'd never fired so much as a .22 pistol.

A voice boomed through the pyramid's PA system. "Attention! Two intruders are in the building. They're wearing Day of the Dead masks and vaquero costumes. They are located on SL1 and are heavily armed. Shoot to kill!"

Any doubts Serrano had about the mission were washed away by the words *Shoot to kill.*

Serrano pointed to the nearest camera. "Destroy every camera you see!"

Colon brought the 12 gauge to bear and fired. The recoil caught the priest by surprise, and he took an involuntary step backwards. But the spread from 9 pellets was sufficient to destroy the camera.

There was no place to hide where they were. And hopefully Pia was up ahead. So that, plus the possibility of cover at her location, made Serrano's decision easy. "Reload the shotgun and follow me."

Serrano drew both pistols as he rounded the corner ahead. Three uniformed guards were running at him. Rather than spread out, they were in a single file.

The lead man fired. Serrano heard the bullets snap past his head, paused to bring the 5-inch pistol up into position, and returned fire.

The first hollow point killed the lead man *and* the asshole behind him. A second bullet took the third guard down. Serrano fired again just to make sure. "Grab a pistol!" Serrano ordered. "And extra ammo if they have it."

Colon hurried to obey as Serrano took a peek around the corner. What he saw looked like a full-on detention facility. Cells lined both walls, six to a side, but it was impossible to see how many were occupied.

A long table was positioned in the middle of the corridor. And, judging from the cards that the guards left behind, they'd been playing a game when the shit hit the fan.

Serrano hoped Pia was in one of the cells. But, regardless, he intended to use a cell for cover. There was a loud boom as Colon destroyed the camera mounted above the tables.

"Pia," Serrano said, as he inspected the cells. "Is she here?"

"Yes!" Colon replied exultantly. "Over here!"

Keys were lying on a table. Serrano grabbed them and hurried over. He could see a woman curled up in a corner. Her hands were covering her ears. "Loud! Too loud!"

Colon rushed to help her. "Pia! It's your father... Get up. This is your chance to leave."

"Your head," Pia said. "It's pulsating. Leave me alone."

"She's on drugs," Serrano said. "Peyote most likely."

Serrano was going to say more, but that was when the backups arrived. Not uniformed guards this time, but self-styled Aztec warriors, armed with axes and spears. Two of them were women. An axe flew through the air to clang against the bars as the attackers prepared to rush Pia's cell.

In order to confront the intruders, the warriors had to crowd through the open door. So, when Serrano fired, the warriors collapsed in a heap. Serrano stepped over their bodies to confront a woman.

Her spear missed. Serrano charged, threw the warrior to the floor, and held her there. The fanatic's eyes were dilated—which suggested that she was on drugs. "Pia... Why is she locked up?"

"Patecatl wants her."

Patecatl wasn't real. But Sebastian Acara was real. And he was known to "channel" Patecatl. So, it stood to reason that Acara was the person who wanted Pia dead.

"*Why?*" Serrano demanded. "Why does Patecatl want Pia?"

"Pia saw something," the woman said dreamily. "Something she wasn't supposed to see. Not until she became a Prime."

Serrano jumped to the obvious conclusion. "Did Pia see a murder?"

"No," the woman replied. "She saw a transference. And tonight, it will be her turn."

Serrano got to his feet. "You can leave. Run."

The warrior struggled to her feet and staggered away.

Colon had Pia on her feet by then. One arm was draped over the priest's shoulders. "Come on," Serrano said. "We've got to get out of here."

"Take her other arm," Colon instructed, as Serrano dropped a moon clip into the long gun. "We'll carry her."

With Pia hanging between them, the men carried Pia around the corner, and toward the elevator. Serrano half expected to see more warriors waiting for them. There weren't any.

The elevator rose smoothly and ground to a stop. The doors clattered open. And there, arrayed in front of them, were eleven men. Sebastian Acara stood out. He was six-three and stripped to the waist. He looked like the body builder that he was.

As Acara opened his mouth to speak, Father Colon released Pia and fired the shotgun. His aim was off, so only five pellets hit their target. But that was sufficient. Acara fell like a tree and landed with an audible thump.

Serrano released Pia as well, brought the 5-inch up, and fanned the custom-made hammer. Four .357 rounds struck their targets, wounding one and killing three.

That left six warriors. Three of them fired. Serrano staggered as a slug hit his right thigh. He nearly fell, but managed to remain vertical, as he pulled Shorty.

Colon had the feel of it by then. *BOOM! Clack. BOOM! Clack. BOOM! Clack.* Warriors fell. And, as the wounded man attempted to stand, Serrano shot him again.

Colon had to step over bodies as he carried Pia to the van.

Serrano left a blood trail behind as he limped over to the guard station and thumbed the up button.

Tires squealed as the van stopped next to Serrano. It took everything the ex-Marine had left to open the door and crawl inside.

Then, as Serrano's head swam, he struggled to pull his belt free, and fashion a tourniquet.

There were more things to do. Serrano knew that... And he was going to tell the priest all about them when darkness pulled him down.

There was pain. A lot of pain as Serrano came to. Blurry faces peered down at him. A man spoke. "The bullet didn't hit bone. And, because it went straight through, I won't have to go in after it. Your Soldado is a lucky man. Change that dressing every six hours. What he needs most is lots of rest. Some Tylenol will help."

Serrano felt a needle prick followed by a return to darkness.

Time passed. Serrano opened his eyes to find that he was lying on a bed in a pleasant room, with sunlight streaming in through a window. Where was he? And where was the bathroom? Serrano performed a sit-up, turned, and felt a stab of pain in his right thigh.

It was bad, but some of the wounds Serrano had suffered previously had been worse. The immediate threat was the distinct possibility that he would pee on the bed.

Serrano clenched his teeth, cradled the leg with his hands, and swung it over onto the floor. Then he stood. The pain produced an involuntary grunt.

A quad cane was there waiting for him. And that's where Serrano was, about to start a journey of exploration, when the door opened and a woman entered. She had dark hair, a sturdy figure, and a maternal manner. "You're up! How do you feel?"

"My thigh hurts, and I need to use a bathroom," Serrano answered. "No offense, but who are you?"

The woman smiled. "My name is Camila. I'm Pia's mother. Thank you for what you did. God knows and he'll reward you. Follow me."

Camila left the room and Serrano followed. The cane was a big help. The bathroom was down the hall on the right. Serrano entered, closed the door, and lifted the toilet seat.

Once he was done Serrano washed his hands and examined his countenance in the mirror. What was that? Three days' worth of beard? Something like that.

Serrano returned to the bedroom to find that a western style shirt and a new pair of Levis were waiting for him. The jeans were a challenge because of the wound but, by taking his time, Serrano managed to pull them on. The sandals were easy to slip on.

The smell of frying tocineta led Serrano to a small, thoughtfully arranged kitchen. "There you are," Camila said. "How do you like your bacon? ¿Roja? ¿O bien cocida?"

"Bien cocido, por favor."

"Have a seat," Camila said. "Help yourself to coffee."

Serrano sat down, poured coffee into a mug, and took a sip. It was excellent. "Where am I anyway?"

"You're in the Iztapalapa neighborhood of Mexico City," Camila answered as she broke two eggs into a pan. "Tomás brought you here."

"Tomás?"

Camila turned to look at Serrano. There was defiance in her eyes.

"Father Colon."

Serrano nodded. "Thanks. And your daughter? How is she?"

Camila turned back to her cooking. "Tomás took Pia to spend some time with the Sisters of the Sun. They specialize in helping addicts. Breakfast is served."

Serrano's stomach growled as Camila placed the food in front of him. "Muchas gracias. I'm hungry."

Camila sat across from him. "Do you mind if I smoke?"

"Nope."

Camila shook a cigarette out of a Marlboro package and lit up. "It's bad for me, like Tomás is bad for me, but I need both of them."

"Tell me about what happened after we left the Foundation."

Camila exhaled a stream of smoke. "All hell broke loose. There were so many bodies that the police suspected that a gang of narcos were responsible. Then, when they opened Acara's walk-in safe and found a huge stash of drugs—not to mention blackmail photos of public officials—that assumption was validated."

"And that's it?"

"No," Camila replied. "After interrogating so-called 'Primes,' the name for members of Acara's inner circle, the police learned that the group had participated in ritual murders." She took a drag off her cigarette and exhaled. "And, according to Pia, that's what was in store for her. They forced her to take drugs as part of the preparation process. So, thank you again. I'm sorry about the gunshot wound."

"De nada. You're a good cook."

"And Martina?" Camila inquired. "Is she a good cook?"

"Martina? You know her?"

"Sí. She calls once a day to check on you. Your phone is in the guest room."

Serrano felt a sense of warmth that had nothing to do with the coffee. *I am*, he reflected, *a lucky man.*

*

Lugar de Paz, Mexico

Weeks had passed since the battle inside the Acara Foundation, and although Serrano's leg was better, he still had a way to go. That's why he was walking in a circle, and doing deep knee bends, while Paco fired his .22 at homemade targets standing on sticks.

The boy was good. Very good. And not just at shooting. Paco was constantly looking for ways to help Martina. And mostly doing his homework.

Paco was good company too, and Serrano looked forward to spending time with the muchacho after school.

Serrano was limping even more after his laps, but that was to be expected, and a natural part of his self-imposed physical therapy program.

Paco was about to reload when Serrano called to him. "That's enough, pistolero. Dinner will be ready soon… And your mother will be unhappy if we're late. Police your brass. And remember to clean your weapon this evening. Or what?"

"Or you'll cut my ammo supply off."

"Exactamente."

"Weird Vicky" wasn't her real name. But that was the moniker that Marlo Kirby was known by in the business. She was prone, on top of the U-shaped rock quarry, watching Serrano through a monocular. *There he is*, Vicky told herself, *a dead man walking.*

Vicky doesn't kill people in front of children. No, she doesn't, Vicky added. *Only bad people do that. Like the ones that did my Pa.*

Vicky don't like Mexico. No, she doesn't. And Mr. Yankovic

wants his money. Yesterday if you please. So, no dick'n around. Not that Vicky has a dick, because she doesn't.

The car pulled away. Vicky rolled over onto her back. A black vulture was circling above. *Vicky ain't dead yet, you sonofabitch.* Then she raised a long-barreled pistol and fired.

The bird seemed to hesitate for a second before spiraling down. The body raised a puff of dust as it landed. Vicky grinned.

Night had fallen. Moonlight cast a ghostly glow over Lugar de Paz as Weird Vicky drove her Zacua electric vehicle into Serrano's neighborhood.

Silence was important because Vicky knew that Serrano had a dog. A yappy Chihuahua that was allowed to roam at night— and was inclined to yap at everything including cars, coyotes and raccoons.

Vicky knew that because she'd been watching Serrano's house via a drone the night before. And now, after spraying herself with Scent-A-Way, Vicky felt sure that she could get close enough to pop the dog with her suppressed .22.

Prior to exiting the vehicle, Vicky put her infrared goggles on, and checked to ensure that they were operational. *Vicky ain't no fool*, she thought. *That's why Vicky is still alive.*

Having disabled the Zacua's dome light earlier, the assassin was able to open the door without triggering the kind of glow that could attract someone's attention.

Then it was a matter of approaching the house and popping the dog. Vicky was wearing old-fashioned high-top sneakers, and they were silent as she ghosted through the murk.

Vicky was close, very close when she saw a green colored Chihuahua lifting a leg over one of the spiky plants in Serrano's yard. The dog was busy covering the pee patch when Vicky shot it. The subsonic .22 cartridge produced a barely audible clack as the dog went down.

Good Vicky, the assassin thought. *It's time to break and enter.*

Vicky had spent six months training to become a locksmith. An investment that had paid off many times over.

The 7-piece pick and hook set was kept ready in a pocket and, thanks to Vicky's expertise, it took less than a minute to open Serrano's front door.

Was it alarmed? No, not as far as Vicky could tell. *Vicky is a lucky ducky*, the hired killer thought. *Fifty large. That's the amount Mr. Yankovic is going to pay Vicky. And Vicky's going to Disneyland.*

The lights were off except for the soft glow emanating from what Vicky assumed to be a bathroom. The door to the adjacent bedroom was slightly ajar. Vicky nudged it open. Thanks to the night vision goggles Vicky could see that someone was lying in bed.

But she could also see what looked like a human form stretched out on the floor beside the bed. One of them was a fake. But which? The solution was obvious: Shoot both.

Serrano was asleep on the steel plate that Emillio and he had laid across the rafters, when Macho limped into the bedroom on three legs, and began to yap.

Vicky was firing into the form on the bed, as Serrano rolled off the sleeping platform, and landed on top of her. The impact drove the killer to the floor and her weapon went flying. There was no mistaking the pressure against the base of Vicky's skull. "Are you alone?"

Vicky considered telling a lie, but knew Serrano would see

through it. If she had sides, they would have entered the bed-room. "Yes, I am."

"Did Mr. Yankovic send you?"

"Yes."

"I can't let you live, because you'll try again."

"Vicky knows that."

"How do you want it?"

Weird Vicky was lying on a sheet of plastic. She knew why. "The back of Vicky's head is fine."

"Vaya con Dios."

Chapter Eight

East of La Antigua, Mexico

It was dark, the Gulf of Mexico was calm, and the bulk carrier *Celene* was creeping along at four knots—less than half of the freighter's top speed. Her running lights were off, lest someone report her presence to authorities, although that was unlikely.

The people who lived along that stretch of coast were used to seeing strange lights at night, hearing the roar of powerful engines, and knew it was best to ignore the contrabandistas.

But Captain Nels Andersen wasn't one to leave things to chance. The stakes were too high for that. The *Celene* was carrying two cargos: concrete and fentanyl.

Of the two cargoes, the fentanyl was the more profitable. So much so, that Andersen and the members of his six-man crew were going to make $100,000 each by dropping a "train" of six water-tight barrels over the side. But $600,000 was nothing. Each container would be worth millions to the Los Ceros cartel.

A light flashed to starboard. Three longs, followed by two blips. Andersen turned to the first mate, a Nigerian named Umar Obi. "Give them the counter signal. And tell the boatswain to lower the ladder. One, and only one, visitor will be permitted to come aboard. If there's more, order the crew to open fire on them, and we'll head out to sea."

Obi had served in the Nigerian navy and liked a bit of formality. "Sir! Yes, sir!"

Andersen grinned, as his number two made his way out onto the starboard bridge wing, and triggered a powerful flashlight.

It wasn't long before powerful engines were heard, and a thirty-five-foot launch came alongside. The boatswain was at the foot of the accommodation ladder, ready to receive a line or repel boarders. Whichever the occasion demanded.

Fortunately, there was no need for gunfire as a young man sporting a backwards ballcap and a black satin jacket ran up the ladder. He was carrying an aluminum overnight case.

Obi took command as Andersen went down to meet their visitor. Neither of them had met before, and neither was interested in social niceties. "Are you ready?" the narco demanded.

"We are," Andersen replied. "The canisters are here, lids off, ready for testing."

"Let's do it," the narco replied, as a large drone appeared overhead. The threat was obvious.

It took less than ten minutes to take samples and test them. All were satisfactory. "Muy bueno," the youngster said, as he gestured to the suitcase. "Revísalo."

Andersen's heart was beating faster as he knelt and opened the case. His headlamp was enough to illuminate the contents.

The trick was to dive deep and make sure the neat stacks of twenties went all the way down. After three spot checks, Andersen was satisfied. "Let's seal the cannisters. It's important to screw the lids on tight."

Though half empty—in order to float—the barrels were heavy. The containers had been roped together to form a "train." One of the ship's derricks was used to hoist up the cargo net full of barrels, swing them out over the port side, and let them go.

A beacon attached to the lead "car" flashed on and off. Once the kid was back on the launch, he took the train in tow, and headed for shore. The *Celene* disappeared into the night.

Los Ceros had a fleet of armored Mercedes G-Class SUVs, costing $200,000 each. Five of them were parked on the sand-drifted parking lot behind the old Albacore Cannery. The vehicles were a reward for those who met their targets, an enticement for street kids, and some flash for everyone else. The Federales included. They were also dead giveaways. With the emphasis on *dead*.

That was what Elena Isabella Ayo, head of the Las Rojas cartel, thought as she took a final look around. *Most of them are looking out to sea*, Ayo thought, *rather than west. Es un regalo de Dios.*

Like all of her soldados, Ayo was wearing a voice-activated headset. "You have your targets, muchachos . Take them down."

The lookout was invisible except for the glow of his carrujo . Ayo drew her compound bow back, took aim, and let go.

The high-tech carbon arrow hissed through the air, struck its target, and killed him instantly. The carrujo landed on the ground.

Ayo hurried forward to stand over the body. Other sentries went down—some sprouting two, or even three, deadly shafts.

La Roja was beginning to believe that her Reds were going to overrun the old cannery when a beam of light shot down through holes in the roof to illuminate all but a few hiding places. Then a 500-pound military grade bomb fell on the complex. The resulting explosion destroyed what remained of the cannery and killed three Reds. The blast wave knocked Ayo off her feet. *A drone!* That's what the cartel leader thought, as she struggled to her feet. *A fucking zumbido.*

How many bombs could the machine carry? One, Ayo guessed. *So now, unless the machine is armed with rockets, it's nothing more than a flying turd.*

But that wasn't true as Ayo soon learned. Thanks to what the drone could "see" from above, the Zeros could target the surviving Reds with sniper fire. A fact that forced them to take cover rather than advance.

Meanwhile, owing to the reports that were coming in, Ayo knew that a launch was approaching shore and that Zs were wading out into the surf. Why? Because they were going to get the fármacos and drag them up onto the beach.

Mateo was a capataz and one of Ayo's most trusted men. "Mateo," Ayo said. "Kill the men in the surf."

The Kawasaki jet skis were waiting half a mile north of the cannery, loitering under a pier. Each machine had a driver and a gunner armed with an HK MP7 machine pistol.

Once Mateo gave the order it was a simple matter to start engines, jettison anchor cords, and head south. There were three machines in all. And there was no way to disguise the combined roar that their engines made. Which meant that the Zeros knew there was some sort of water craft about to arrive.

But even the drone operator had a hard time spotting the jet skis until they neared the cannery, and by then it was too late. Suddenly the machines were in among the Zeros, guns firing, as the drivers uttered personal war cries.

Some of the Zs tried to swim out to sea. Others attempted to reach the beach. But regardless of which way they went, the unique penetrators that the HKs fired found them.

And it wasn't long before the incoming waves were red. And *that*, La Roja decided, was how it should be.

*

La Hacienda Roja, south of Paso del Toro, Mexico

Three days had passed since the battle with Los Ceros. Bodies had been buried. Significant sums of money had been paid to bereaved families, assorted Federales, and members of the local judiciary. And the fentanyl was being processed for distribution.

In order to celebrate what Las Rojas called *a new beginning*, a party was being held at the Ayo family's sprawling hacienda. There was non-stop music from two mariachi bands, pony rides for the children, and plenty of refreshments for their parents.

But in spite of the gaiety there were somber notes, too. Like the tethered spy balloons which floated above, the snipers stationed on lookout towers, and the empty-eyed servants—prisoners "on loan" from José Coro—the district court judge for that area.

And there to make sure that the prisoners behaved themselves, was Señora Flores, a strict disciplinarian who had the power to administer corporal punishment if needed.

Guests danced, the bands played, and Ayo was everywhere. She thanked people, told stories, and kissed babies. All of which was part of her effort to foster what she called *nuestra familia*. That is, an organization held together by more than money.

Finally, as guests began to depart, Ayo brought the most important members of the "family" together in what had been her husband's spacious study. It was a room replete with family photos, antique ranching paraphernalia, and shelves of leather-bound books. Because the study was located in the oldest part of the house, there were no windows. Only rifle slits.

Ayo's sons Ricardo, Mateo, and Benito—often referred to as El Niño—were there. As were the hacienda's foremen Mateo and Camilo.

La Raja raised a glass of wine pressed from the family's vineyard. "To all of my boys, living and dead. God bless you!" There was a pause while the men nodded and sipped their drinks.

"Now," Ayo said. "A great victory has been won. The leaders of Los Ceros were killed. And, under Ricardo's leadership, their territory will merge with ours. No small accomplishment.

"But is that enough? No! Of course not. What your father envisioned was a full-fledged country within a country. What some might call a narco state. But I reject that label because of the negative connotations associated with it." All those present had heard versions of the speech before, but did their best to look interested.

"So," Ayo continued. "We can't rest. We must grow. And do it quickly before the pendejos in Mexico City realize what's taking place and send the Marines in.

"So that, my darlings, is why we are going to attack Los Caribes, kill El Cuchillo, and add his territory to ours."

That was new. And very, very dangerous. The brothers exchanged glances but remained silent. It was Mateo who raised his glass. "*A la victoria!*"

Rancho del Sol, Mexico

It was dark and a powerful flashlight lit the scene. The calf's forelegs were sticking straight out. But its hindquarters had collapsed. It *mooed* pitifully.

The veterinarian shook his head sadly. No one liked to deliver bad news to El Cuchillo. "I'm sorry, Señor Ramierz, but we'll have to put her down."

Ramirez had heard of mad cow disease. And read about it. So, he knew that bovine spongiform encephalopathy was a fatal neurologic disease. Furthermore, Ramirez was aware that the condition was transmitted by an abnormal prion protein found in contaminated feed.

And since Ramierz purchased all his feed from Héctor Delgado in the nearby town of Llera, he was seething with anger and struggled to hide it from the vet. "So, all the calves will have to be put down?"

"Yes, unless you know which cow gave birth to it."

Unfortunately, Ramirez didn't know because his stock ran free. And he was about to say as much when the clatter of helicopter rotors was heard. At least two but maybe three.

The helos passed overhead and made straight for the well-lit house in the distance. Ramirez felt an emptiness in the pit of his stomach. La Roja. It had to be her. She was the only cartel leader who had a small air force.

Ramirez brought the radio up to his lips. "Code Red. Destroy the incoming aircraft. Prepare to engage enemy troops on the ground."

Then Ramirez turned to his driver. "Bruno, get me to the house, and step on it."

The Range Rover drove away. The vet and sick cow were left behind.

As her helicopters attacked El Cuchillo's house, Elena Ayo was inbound, aboard her family's aging Cessna 208B Grand Caravan plane.

The 208 had a high wing, large door, and two benches for skydivers to sit on. The port cargo hatch had been converted into a roll-up door for skydiving. And fourteen armed jumpers followed Ayo as she threw herself out of the plane.

The Cessna was at 5,000 feet, which was low by normal standards, so the Rojas would be able to reach the ground quickly.

Even so, Ayo had a brief moment in which to enjoy the instant when one of her helicopters dropped an incendiary device on El Cuchillo's house. It exploded into flames that quickly spread.

Ayo flinched as a surface-to-air missile fired from a man-portable air-defense system struck the helo and destroyed it.

But the ground was coming up fast, and she had to focus on that rather than the loss of a helicopter and two pilots.

The light thrown by the burning house was enough to see by. Ayo took aim at the green astroturf in front of El Cuchillo's home and, by making use of the parachute's control toggles, was able to flare in. After Ayo's boots made contact, she was forced to take three steps forward, before coming to a full stop.

Thanks to practice and quick release fasteners, La Roja shed the chute quickly, and spoke into her mike. "Form on me. Remember, our goal is to find El Cuchillo and kill him, so stay focused. Let's go."

"Skydivers have landed," a member of Ramirez's team announced. "And they're closing in on the house. Over."

This is an assassination attempt, not a raid, Ramirez reasoned. *And there's no way to save the house. So, it's time to use plan D.*

"Pull back," Ramirez ordered. "You have thirty seconds to clear zone A. Start the countdown, Balasco. Over."

Ayo could tell that something was wrong. Rather than engage her Reds, the Knives were pulling back away from the fiery inferno. *Why?*

Because she and her men were in a trap, that's why. Ayo turned her back to the blaze and yelled, "Run!"

The narcos ran. And were still running when the command-detonated mines began to explode. They'd been planted two years earlier for use as a last-stand defensive screen. And, while the explosions destroyed the house, the tradeoff was worth it.

Ayo and three of her fastest runners escaped, as dozens of deafening blasts circled the fully engulfed mansion—and tore the slower Rojas asunder. Body parts were hurled in every direction. Some disappeared into the pyre, others landed on the grounds, waiting to be discovered the following morning.

Ayo had one card left to play, and that was helo two, which was still aloft. The cartel leader was running full tilt as she ordered the helicopter to land near the ranch's water tower. It, ironically, was crowned with a flashing beacon to prevent low-flying aircraft from hitting it.

The little helo wasn't designed to carry four people, but they entered nevertheless, and the pilot managed to lift. Not far, only a hundred feet or so, but enough to flee the area.

In the meantime, there was nothing Ramirez could do except light a cigar from one of the burning splinters that littered his cactus garden. The fire crackled and a host of sparks spiraled up into the night sky. What was the old proverb? *Revenge is best served cold?*

Yes, Ramirez decided. But *how?*

Chapter Nine

Highway 49, headed for Juan Aldama, Mexico

Serrano was happy. Or, as happy as he could be. The weather was good. Martina was next to him, her head on a pillow, taking a nap. And, after hassling Serrano about the hitwoman's death, the Federales had cleared him.

The issue from their perspectives was the nature of her head wound. Serrano's bullet had entered the back of the Americana's skull from only inches away. That was obvious. So, how could Serrano claim self-defense?

"She was firing at what she thought was my body," Serrano explained, "as I rolled off my elevated sleeping platform and landed on top of her.

"She fell facedown, my pistol discharged accidentally, and the bullet struck the back of her head. That was unfortunate, but I can't say that I'm sorry."

"Alright," a sergeant named Otero said wearily. "She was trying to kill you. That's true. But why do so many people want you dead?"

Serrano frowned and shook his head. "I wish I knew." And that was the end of it as far as Otero was concerned.

But not for Mr. Yankovic. Serrano had miscalculated. Originally, after stealing Yankovic's money, Serrano figured the bastard would give up attempting to recover it after a couple of tries. But he was still at it. *Maybe he'll give up now*, Serrano thought. *I hope so.*

Martina stirred, sat up, and rubbed her eyes. "Where are we?"

"About halfway there," Serrano answered.

Martina smiled. "I love you."

"And I love you," Serrano replied.

Serrano had been the first to use the L-word a few days earlier, and had no regrets about doing so. But now, in keeping with the new stage in their relationship, Martina was taking him home to meet her parents. A trial Serrano wasn't looking forward to, but understood the need for, since the possibility of marriage loomed ahead. They hadn't discussed it yet, but Serrano knew it would come up soon.

Juan Aldama was nestled among some dry hills, and was comprised of low one- and two-story buildings, some of which bore tropical hues.

The town struck Serrano as a sleepy place, even if it was named after a famous insurgent and served as the local seat of government.

The Escalera home was modest but well maintained. A three-foot-high wire mesh fence served to protect a lush vegetable garden from free range dogs, rambunctious children, and wandering farm animals. Especially goats.

Señora Escalera was working in the garden when they arrived and hurried out to embrace her only child. "Martina! You're so thin… We'll work on that. And this is the man you told us about. The one they call El Soldado. Welcome home, Nick."

"It's a pleasure to meet you, Señora. Martina talks about you all the time."

"Please, call me Rosa," Señora Escalera replied. "Bring your things inside. That's where Juan is, watching a football game."

When the visitors appeared, Juan turned the TV off, stood, and came forward to shake hands. Serrano noticed that the bricklayer's hands were callused, his skin was a deep brown color from years in the sun, and his eyes were bright with intelligence.

"I see that you're heavily armed. That makes sense in Lugar de Paz. But not here. Juan Aldama is relatively peaceful."

Serrano took the hint, removed the rig, and hung it on a peg. "I'm glad to hear that. We have problems, but thanks to Martina and her fighters, the situation is better than it would be otherwise."

"There will be no talk about bad things while you're here," Rosa insisted.

"Juan, take Nick to the playhouse. It's out back," Rosa explained. "Juan built it for Martina. It's small, but it has a perfectly good bed, and you'll be comfortable there."

Martina had warned Serrano about how devout her parents were, so he knew they wouldn't be sleeping together. The playhouse was well crafted but small.

Serrano had to bend over to pass through the door, and the bed was no more than five feet long, which meant that his lower legs and feet would protrude beyond the homemade mattress. The solution was obvious. Serrano would sleep the way he usually did. On the floor.

The rest of the day was spent on the well-shaded veranda drinking cold Coronas, nibbling on the seemingly endless antojitos that Rosa brought from her kitchen, and reviewing Martina's many accomplishments. Those included being the first member of the family to earn a college degree, a dozen awards for singing, and giving birth to the perfect child who, according to Rosa, was overdue for a visit.

What was missing from the list—to Serrano's way of thinking—was Martina's bravery, and her leadership in fighting Los Caribes, the cartel responsible for her husband's death.

But according to what Martina had told him, those were forbidden subjects, because her parents disapproved of her role as a guerilla fighter.

So, the day passed pleasantly. Rosa prepared a wonderful dinner, and Serrano did his best to entertain his hosts with Marine Corps stories. The funny kind rather than anything related to combat.

Bedtime came early in the Escalera house, and that was just fine with Serrano, who was tired. Martina kissed him on the lips in front of her parents, winked at him, and withdrew to what had once been her bedroom.

After a round of "Good nights," Serrano made his way out to the playhouse where he moved the bedding to the floor. It was chilly, so Serrano went to bed with his clothes on.

Sleep came quickly, and Serrano was dead to the world when Martina burst into the room sobbing. She immediately sat down on the bed, head bowed, shoulders heaving.

Serrano hurried to exit the mummy bag before going to sit next to her. One arm went around her shoulders. "What's wrong, cariño?"

"Everything," Martina said between sobs. "Carmen called me. El Cuchillo's narcos attacked Lugar de Paz. Our guerillas fought them off, but three were killed. Paco's paternal grandmother Yaya was one of them. She tried to keep the bastardas out of my house, but they broke in, and shot her. Then they took Paco and left. I'm going to kill Ramirez."

Serrano felt all sorts of emotions. Sorrow regarding Yaya. Fear for Paco. And a deep abiding anger. "I get that, baby, but El Cuchillo's pistoleros would kill you long before you could get anywhere near the bastard. And what happens to Paco then?

"Let's stall, and if we're going to go in with guns blazing, let's bring some help."

Martina nodded, but Serrano could tell that she wasn't convinced.

They packed quickly and hit the road. Rosa was crying, and Juan was trying to comfort her, as Martina and Serrano departed.

They were clear of Juan Aldama when Martina's phone chimed. The call was from Martina's friend Carmen.

Martina listened, glanced at Serrano, and switched to speakerphone. "Nick is here beside me. Tell him what you told me."

"The narcos left a note," Carmen said. "It says that El Cuchillo will slit Paco's throat unless you come to see him. And it says that you should leave your guns behind."

"It sounds as if El Cuchillo knows how I feel about Paco," Serrano said. "And he thinks I have more money than Martina does. If that's the case, I'll pay every peso I have to get our boy back."

Martina reached over to squeeze Serrano's thigh. Tears were running down her cheeks.

The rest of the trip was spent discussing *what ifs*, and wondering about Paco. Had he been injured? Were the narcos feeding the boy? Was he scared?

It was wasted energy for the most part, but Serrano knew it was a process that Martina had to go through, even if it was fruitless.

Damage from the narco attack was clear to see as Serrano and Martina drove through town. Windows had been shattered by gunfire, the truck that had been used to rob the local Savings & Loan was still half buried in the lobby, and the municipal building had been fire bombed.

Martina's home was largely untouched, as was Serrano's, and Macho was there to greet him. Even though the Chihuahua had only three legs, he was just as aggressive as he'd been before, and Serrano paused to pet him.

Serrano and Martina had agreed that it didn't make sense to try and meet with Ramirez with night coming on. It would be better to do so in the morning.

Serrano spent a sleepless night tossing and turning rather than sleeping and arose feeling tired. He wasn't particularly hungry, but forced himself to eat a piece of toast before leaving.

The Rancho del Sol was about thirty miles away. Serrano felt a horrible emptiness in the pit of his stomach. What if El Cuchillo demanded more money than he had? What would he do then? And what if the drug lord wanted to kill him?

Then I'll be dead, Serrano concluded. *End of story.*

The first layer of security was the roofed guard station located at the point where the two-lane highway intersected with a gravel road. A man wearing a cowboy hat and western gear flagged Serrano down. He was armed with an AR-15.

"Señor Ramirez is expecting you, but we're under orders to search the car. Get out." Serrano had no choice but to obey.

There were two guards and they spent a full fifteen minutes searching the car and Serrano. Finally, after inspecting the underside of the Taurus with a mirror mounted on a pole, they allowed Serrano to proceed.

It didn't take Serrano long to realize that Rancho del Sol was a real working ranch rather than a plot of ground with a pretentious name.

Cattle were visible on the left, with horses to the right. Well maintained fences kept both from straying.

The second security stop was less stringent than the first, but a guard entered the car, and sat in the passenger seat as Serrano passed the blackened remains of a helicopter.

And, further on, the burned wreckage of what had been a sprawling house could be seen. Serrano was ordered to stop in front of what looked like a new motorhome.

It was obvious to Serrano's trained eye that a substantial battle had been fought at Rancho del Sol, and that El Cuchillo was the loser.

Serrano was ordered out of the car, told to "Assume the position," so he could be searched yet again. He stood with feet spread, and his hands on the Taurus.

"My name is Balasco," a man with a mustache said. "You will follow me."

Balasco led Serrano to an open-sided tent that had been erected next to the motorhome. A man was seated inside. He was wearing a black cowboy hat with a silver band. His eyes were little more than slits. And he exuded authority. "I'm Pablo Ramirez," the drug lord said, without getting up. "Have a seat."

It was an order rather than a suggestion. Serrano obeyed.

"So," Ramirez said. "You're the man they call El Soldado."

Serrano shrugged. "I've been called a lot of things."

Ramirez smiled. His teeth were even and very white. "Haven't we all. Let's get down to business. I have the boy. And, according to what I've been told, you're close to Paco and his mother."

"I am," Serrano agreed. "And I want to see him. Otherwise, this conversation is over."

Ramirez placed a revolver on the table. "I could kill you."

"You could," Serrano said. "But you won't. You summoned me for a reason."

"Balasco," Ramirez said conversationally. "Get the boy."

"Do you smoke?" Ramirez inquired conversationally, as Balasco left.

"No," Serrano replied. "It's bad for your health."

"Well, I do," Ramirez said as he lit a cigar. "Tell me something, El Soldado, why do so many people want to kill you?"

"A lot of people ask me that," Serrano replied. "And the answer is simple. I have a tendency to piss people off."

"Nick!" Paco exclaimed, as he ran forward. "You came! Can we leave now? I don't like it here."

Serrano wrapped the boy in his arms and hugged him. "It's good to see you, son. Are you okay? Do they feed you?"

Paco nodded. "Yes, but I want Mamá."

"And she wants you," Serrano replied. "We'll get you out of here as soon as we can."

Paco burst into tears as Balasco led him away.

"So," Ramirez said. "I've seen it with my own eyes."

"You've seen what?"

"How much you care about the boy."

"Let's dispense with the bullshit," Serrano replied. "You took Paco. What will it cost to get him back?"

"This isn't about money," El Cuchillo responded, as he blew a smoke ring.

"Then what's it about?"

"If you want to free Paco, all you have to do is kill Elena Isabella Ayo, otherwise known as La Roja. It's a simple matter for El Soldado," Ramirez said. "Bang. She's dead."

It was not a simple matter. Because, if it was, Ramirez would have ordered one of his narcos to do it. Serrano remembered the charred remains of a house. "Ayo burned your house down."

Ramirez nodded. "Yes, she did. So, kill her and the boy goes free."

"How do I know you'll keep your word?"

"Because I'm an honest man. Ask anyone."

El Cuchillo was anything but an honest man. But somehow,

in this case, Serrano thought he would be. "And if I kill Ayo, and I'm killed in the process, then what?"

"Paco will be returned to his mother. Who I will kill later on."

"And if I try, but fail?" Serrano inquired.

"Then Martina Blanco's son will arrive home in a coffin," Ramirez said coldly.

There was a long moment of silence, followed by Serrano's answer. "Okay, I'll do it. But don't expect overnight results. This will take time."

Ramirez nodded. "I understand. This meeting is over. Feel free to leave."

How the hell will you do it? That was the thought that dominated Serrano's thoughts, as Serrano returned to Martina's home. He gave it to her straight, and Martina burst into tears. "No! I won't hear of it. I don't want that. And Paco wouldn't want that."

Serrano took Martina into his arms. "Paco is eight years old. And what he wants is his mamá. Don't worry. This is my skill. It's the only thing I'm good for. I'll find a way. And I'll set Paco free."

Serrano went from Martina's house to the church, where he found Father Colon mopping a floor. The priest stopped. "How much? How much money will we have to raise?"

"None, Father. All I have to do is kill someone and El Cuchillo will set Paco free."

"Kill someone? That's a mortal sin."

"Yes," Serrano agreed. "But remember when I confessed? And my penance? You ordered me to protect Lugar la Paz from evil. And that's what I plan to do."

Colon made the sign of the cross. "I say foolish things sometimes. Who is it?"

"Elena Isabella Ayo. La Roja."

Colon crossed himself again. "I will forgive you if you survive. And, I will pray for you when you die."

"Thanks for the vote of confidence," Serrano said. "I need your help."

"Anything," Colon said. "Name it."

"I know you're in touch with dozens of priests and lay people. Tap into your network for me. Find a narco who used to work for La Roja and is willing to brief me about her operation. I'll pay a thousand U.S. dollars."

After a moment, Serrano cautioned, "This person will have to be under lock and key until my mission is over however. Otherwise, he might go to Ayo and get me killed."

Colon put the mop aside. "I'll get to work. What are you going to do?"

"I'm going to take a trip to Agua Frio," Serrano answered. "That's where the Ayo family lives, right?"

"That's the closest town to La Roja's hacienda," Colon agreed. "Be careful. Ayo owns Agua Frio and everyone in it."

It was a 50-mile drive to Agua Frio. Serrano spent the first 40 worrying. Then, as he drew closer, Serrano forced himself to focus. The first thing that caught his attention was a roadside billboard with the smiling countenance of Elena Isabella Ayo on it.

Ayo had reddish hair, appeared to be forty something, and was urging motorists to stop in the town of Agua Frio, "Where the water is cool, and our hearts are warm."

What a load of bullshit. But Serrano knew that some people would buy it. And the supersized La Roja was a reminder of the task in front of him. Ayo was a big deal. Killing her would be tough.

Serrano felt a stab of fear when he was about five miles from town, and a gun truck appeared in his rearview mirror. Did the narcos know? Were they after him?

A horn blared as the fully loaded truck passed and a narco flipped him off.

What was notable, to Serrano anyway, was the light machine gun mounted over the cab. That would never fly in an area where the Federales were active. Clear evidence that Father Colon was correct. Ayo *did* own everyone in the area.

One pass through Agua Frio. That was all Serrano could allow himself. He might be noticed otherwise. And, worse yet, remembered.

Agua Frio was a storybook town. It wasn't what Serrano expected after the encounter with the gun truck. The buildings were painted in alternating tropical colors. The signs were in the same font. Flower baskets dangled from retro street lamps. And the main drag was scrupulously clean. That said a lot about Ayo.

She's an idealist, Serrano decided. *And a control freak. Not to mention a very ambitious person. The attack on Rancho del Sol is proof of that.*

As Serrano left town, he passed a cyclone fence. It was topped with razor wire and hung with a sign that read: *Carcel de Agua Frio.*

Identical tents were visible beyond, all neat and tidy, with only a few inmates in sight. *Where are the rest of them?* Serrano wondered. *And that's a whole lot of tents for such a small community.*

From there Serrano followed the highway along the bottom of a dry hill. And, when a turnoff appeared, he took it. The one lane, gravel road zigzagged upward to a cell tower and a stone equipment shed.

Broken glass glittered in the sun as Serrano got out of the

car. There were condoms too, which suggested that the hilltop was used for parties. By highschoolers? Narcos? Or both?

Serrano brought Papá's binoculars up to his eyes. He was looking at the Ayo family's hacienda. It was a sight to see. There were green fields, orchards, and roads on a grid. And in the far distance, a sprawling house was visible.

A water tank and the corrals were located next to a private airstrip where a helicopter and two planes were parked. The whole thing was very impressive.

But what worried Serrano most were the white blimps that hovered over the hacienda. They were tethered to masts and sure to be loaded with automated cameras and sensors.

So, could he hike in or crawl in without being detected? No.

Could he shoot Aya from the hilltop he was standing on? No. The range was too great. What did that leave?

Serrano lowered the glasses. He was stumped. But, come hell or highwater, he'd find a way.

Chapter Ten

Near San Luis Potosí, Mexico

Serrano was halfway to Lugar de Paz when Father Colon called. "I found the person you're looking for," Colon said. "Meet me at Saint Anthony's in Valle de Oro."

Serrano pulled over in order to check the nav app on his phone. He wanted to go home. He wanted to see Martina. But time was of the essence.

So, he was forced to go back. Ten miles down the road Serrano saw the Valle de Oro sign, slowed, and made the necessary turn.

The sun was in Serrano's eyes as he followed the two-lane highway through foothills, across a bone-dry flat, and through a narrow pass into a valley. The Valley of Gold. But that was more than a hundred years ago.

Since then, many of the buildings along main street had been remodeled, and in some cases repurposed, like the bank which had been converted to a restaurant.

Saint Anthony's sat at the end of the main drag, at the intersection where main street split into First and Second Avenues. The church was an imposing structure with a tiled roof, a spire, and a cross on top.

The sun was setting as Serrano placed the rig in the trunk of the car, locked the doors, and made his way over to the entrance of the church.

As Serrano entered, he saw Colon. The priest was watching a mass and turned to look. Serrano went forward to greet him. They embraced. "Father Olmo gave us the use of his study," Colon announced.

"Your source is a novice, who was employed by the Ayo family before being raped by Benito, La Roja's youngest son. A vicious animal known as El Niño. He's Ayo's favorite and can do no wrong.

"So, when our informer accused him of rape, El Niño claimed that he'd been seduced, and his mother believed him. Ayo's narcos dumped the girl next to the highway like so much trash. Sister Maria is still recovering. So be gentle."

Colon led Serrano into the side corridor which provided access to the sacristy, a meeting room, and a study. That's where Sister Maria was waiting. A transparent veil covered her head, her hands were folded in her lap. Serrano could see why El Niño had been attracted to her. Sister Maria was beautiful.

She rose as the men entered. "Sister Maria," Colon said. "This is the man I told you about. He would like to ask you some questions about the Ayo family and their hacienda. I'll leave you two alone."

Colon withdrew. Serrano invited Sister Maria to sit, and chose a chair across from her. The young woman seemed uncertain at first. But once she realized how mundane Serrano's questions were, she became more voluble. Bit by bit, Serrano drew her out.

At La Hacienda Roja everything was dictated by Elena Isabella Ayo, ranging from major financial decisions all the way down to the way the dining room table was set.

Her sons Ricardo and Mateo did as they were told and ran the day-to-day drug operation, while Benito spent most of his time posing, drinking, and womanizing. Activities that his mother pretended to be unaware of.

Employees were divided into three groups. The narcos sold drugs, kidnapped people, and ran the family's protection rackets. They were young, violent, and often users themselves.

Roughly half of the household staff were people like Sister Maria, who were hired to perform certain tasks such as bookkeeping, aviation, and maintenance.

Sister Maria had been Aya's social secretary, in charge of arranging formal dinners, parties and the bullfights held to entertain so-called "clients." Meaning suppliers and second echelon dealers.

Finally, there was the more numerous group that the Ayos referred to as prestamistas. They were prisoners "on loan" from José Ortega, the local district court judge, who was on the take.

That was when Serrano felt a glimmer of hope. He would never be able to infiltrate the narcos, or be hired to coordinate parties, but he might be able to access the hacienda as a prestamista.

As the conversation came to an end Serrano offered the novice an envelope. "This is a thousand dollars, Sister. For your time. Please don't speak of this meeting to anyone."

"I promise," Sister Maria said. "But I don't want the money."

"Okay," Serrano replied. "But what about the church? Surely Father Olmo could use the money to do God's work."

Sister Maria accepted the envelope. Their eyes locked. "Are you going to harm the Ayo family?"

"Yes."

Sister Maria nodded and said, "Good. Make them pay." And, with that, she left the room.

Serrano stared into space. He had a decision to make. He could go home, see Martina, and try to sleep. Or he could save time by taking immediate action.

Father Colon entered the room. "How did it go?"

"Well," Serrano replied. "Sister Maria was very helpful."

"So, what are you going to do now?"

Serrano told him. Colon was visibly disturbed. "You will be in great danger, my son. Shouldn't you think this over?"

"I have," Serrano replied. "Paco is a prisoner. I must free him. I'm going to give you my wallet. The guns are locked in the trunk of my car. Can you get it to my house? And give me a ride to Agua Frio?"

"Of course I can," the priest said. "Kneel. We must pray."

Serrano had never been any good at praying. Just doing. But he knelt, let Colon do the talking, and hoped that God was listening.

It was dark by the time the two men left. Colon was driving an old KIA. Neither man felt like talking. So, they were mostly silent during the trip. Eventually Agua Frio's lights appeared, and Serrano ordered Colon to pull over. "Who knows what kind of technology the Ayos have installed here. Let's keep your car off their radar. Tell Martina I'm working on it. Tell her I love her."

And with that Serrano got out, turned his back on the KIA, and started to walk. His luggage consisted of an old blanket Father Olmo had contributed, a canvas bag with half a bottle of tequila in it, and some candy bars. The sort of kit that a vagabundo might have.

It took fifteen minutes to reach town. The streetlights were on, and with the exception of two cantinas and a modest hotel, everything was closed.

Judging from the mix of off-road vehicles and sleek sedans parked outside the Dos Amigos bar, it was a favorite of the local narcos, and the perfect place to get in trouble.

Serrano climbed a couple of steps, pushed a swinging door

open, and found himself in a large room. The smell of marijuana hung in the air, a South American soccer game was playing on the big screen TV, and pop music was competing with the game.

No one looked Serrano's way because every eye was on the arm-wrestling match taking place at the center table, where two narcos were going at it. Biceps bulged as bets were placed, backers shouted encouragement, and a half naked waitress served drinks.

Serrano spotted a tiny table with one chair in a corner, and walked a weaving course in that direction, as any drunk might. It wasn't long before the waitress stopped by. "So, hon, what's it going to be?"

"A Corona," Serrano replied. "Gracias."

"That'll be 40 pesos."

"Forty!" Serrano said loudly. "That's bullshit! Do I look stupid?"

A big man appeared as if out of thin air. "Yes," he said, "you do. Now, pay or get out."

Serrano stood, swayed as if inebriated, and steadied himself. "Get out? I just arrived."

Then he took a swing. The bouncer blocked it, punched Serrano in the jaw, and knocked him to the floor. Then the lights went out as the metal-capped toe of a cowboy boot hit the side of his head. The plan was working.

Serrano awoke to discover that his head hurt, he was cold, and lying on a cot. His right hand went up to the wound and found a bandage. And, from the feel of it, there might be stitches too.

Part of Serrano wanted to remain where he was, staring at the roof of what must be a tent. But another part of him wanted to pee, explore, and find something to eat.

Serrano threw the single blanket to one side, swung his boots over onto to the gravel floor, and felt a stab of pain. It took the better part of a minute for it to subside. That was when Serrano realized there were other cots, five of them, four of which were occupied.

Carcel de Agua Frio. That's where Serrano was. And, that's where he wanted to be. Sort of.

Serrano forced himself to stand, and heard gravel crunch under his boots as he left the tent. The sun was just starting to break with the horizon, and a sign pointed the way to el baño.

A concrete path led to a cinderblock building which housed a six-man shower, four urinals, and two sinks. The glare from the fluorescent lights made Serrano wince.

A ceiling mounted camera whirred as he stood in front of a urinal. A surefire way to eliminate fights, sex acts, and sub rosa commerce.

Serrano was washing his hands when a klaxon sounded, and a voice was heard over the P.A. system. "All prisoners will fold their blankets, hit the showers, and report to the cocina al aire libre. Move it."

Serrano didn't have soap, a towel, or clean clothes, so he followed the signs to the cocina and was the first to arrive. There was a coffee urn, eggs served on metal pie plates, and box lunches for later in the day.

Serrano took his share, carried his food to a remote picnic table, and sat down. Other inmates filtered in soon thereafter, and one of them made a beeline to Serrano's table. "Hi! I'm Chico... What's your name?"

Chico, if that was his name, appeared to be in his early twenties. And, despite his cheerful demeanor, was festooned with what Serrano took to be gang tattoos.

So, what was Chico? A friendly kid? A jailhouse hustler?

Or a spy, acting on behalf of the management? Serrano was inclined to put his money on option three. Assuming that was correct, Chico could be used to plant Serrano's cover story. He summoned a smile. "I'm Alberto Esteban. My friends call me Beto."

"Welcome to the circus," Chico said. "We call it that because of the tents, the animals, and the clowns."

Serrano couldn't help but laugh. "So, what's the scoop? Will they put me in front of a judge?"

"Yes, they will," Chico answered. "Judge Coro is stern but reasonable. All you have to do is keep your mouth shut, do your time, and move on. That's what I'm going to do."

None of that lined up with what Sister Maria had told him. So, Serrano's suspicions were confirmed. He nodded. "Gracias, Chico... I appreciate the guidance. Go along to get along. That's what I always say."

The klaxon sounded again and Chico stood. "I have to go. A guard will track you down. Do what he says. Hasta luego."

Chico's words proved to be prophetic when a guard appeared ten minutes later and made his way over to Serrano. "Prisoner Esteban? Follow me."

Serrano tried to keep a straight face. Only one person knew him as Alberto Esteban. And that was Chico. "Yes, sir. Shall I return my plate, sir?"

"Yes," the guard replied. "Take it over to the return window."

Serrano complied, followed the guard, and was led through a maze of passageways to the point where a police van was waiting. Two men and a woman were chained inside. Serrano joined them, was secured in place, and forbidden to speak.

The other inmates were clearly under the same restriction, because the ten-minute journey was made in total silence. The courthouse was a modest one-story building with nothing more than a sign and a Mexican flag to distinguish it from the laundromat next door.

After being released from the van and fitted with leg irons, they were led to a side door that opened into a wire mesh cage. It looked out onto a courtroom. There was a raised bench to the right, tables in front of that, and roughly thirty seats for onlookers. They were empty.

Fifteen minutes passed. Then two men appeared from the left, took their places at the tables, and began to chat with each other. Prosecutor and defense attorney? If so, they seemed to be on extremely good terms.

Another five minutes passed. A policeman appeared. "All rise for District Judge José Coro."

The prisoners were already standing, but the lawyers rose, and continued to stand until Coro was seated.

A clerk had entered. She read a name, one of the other men was released into the courtroom, and ordered to speak in a loud clear voice. "Are you Manuel Pérez?"

"Sí."

"Did you steal apples from the Ayo farm?"

"Sí."

Then and only then did Coro speak. "Señor Pérez, you are hereby sentenced to six months of hard labor. Next."

At no point had either lawyer done anything other than twiddle a pen and sip water. They were clearly window dressing, a nod towards certain laws, while Coro processed the latest batch of prestamistas.

Serrano's alter ego was called next. Serrano, a.k.a. Esteban, left the cage as Pérez returned. The clerk spoke. "What is your name?"

"Alberto Esteban."

"Your file says you don't have any ID. Why?

" I got drunk, and a man hit me. When I woke up my wallet was gone."

"The court will accept that name on a provisional basis, while the police attempt to recover your wallet," Coro announced. "You're charged with public drunkenness and disorderly conduct. Are you innocent or guilty?"

"Guilty."

Coro nodded. "You are sentenced to six months of hard labor. Next."

It seemed that six months was the length of time that Coro and Elena Ayo had agreed on. Once the others had been processed, the inmates were transported back to the jail and were put to work cleaning bathrooms and emptying trash cans. "Enjoy your day off," a guard said. "You'll have to work tomorrow."

Lugar de Paz, Mexico

It was Saturday, and Martina was at home doing chores, when the narco knocked on her door. She held Serrano's derringer down along her right leg. "Yes?"

"I have a message," the boy announced. "From El Cuchillo."

Martina accepted the envelope and ripped it open. The drug lord's handwriting was surprisingly legible:

Señora Blanco,
If you would like to chat and spend some time with your son, please be at the Rancho del Sol at 2 PM.
Sincerely yours,
Pablo Enrique Ramirez

Paco! A chance to visit Paco! Her heart leapt with joy.
But Ramirez wanted to chat. *Why?*

Anticipation was mixed with fear as Martina drove to the ranch, worked her way through the checkpoints, and arrived at the site where the Ramirez house had been.

The charred wreckage was gone. Stakes connected by yellow string marked the outline of a new residence which, judging from stacks of lumber, would be constructed soon.

An open-sided tent was located next to a shiny motorhome, and that's where Ramirez was waiting for her. He stood. "Welcome to Rancho del Sol, señora. I'm Pablo Ramirez. We've never met before. But we know each other in a way that only enemies can. ¿Sí?"

"Sí," Martina replied.

"Please," Ramirez said, as he gestured to a chair. "Have a seat? It's quite warm. Can I offer you a cold lemonade? Iced Tea? Or a Coke?"

"A glass of iced tea would be welcome," Martina replied. "Assuming it isn't poisoned."

Ramirez chuckled. "No. I shall drink from the same pitcher that you do. Besides, we share a common cause. We want Nick Serrano to succeed."

Balasco arrived with a pitcher of iced tea, poured, and faded into the background. Ramirez took a sip. Martina did likewise. "So," Ramirez said. "What, if anything, have you heard from Señor Serrano?"

"Nothing," Martina replied. "But he told me to expect that. Getting close to La Roja won't be easy."

"No," Ramirez agreed. "It won't be. So, tell me Señora, how will our little war end?"

"One of us is going to die," Martina said. "And I hope it's you."

Ramirez nodded. "I understand. But consider this, Señora. I have no children. When I die, the Ayo family is likely to fill the vacuum." He took another sip from his glass. "You are an educated woman. A teacher. So, you've read Homer's Odyssey, and know that Odysseus chose to sail past Scylla, a monster with six heads and shark-like teeth. Why? Because she was the lesser of two evils. Perhaps you should think of me as Scylla."

Martina was both surprised and amused. "So, Elena Ayo is Charybdis. The giant whirlpool that destroys everything in its path three times a day."

Ramirez nodded. "I knew you would understand."

"Even though I'm reluctant to agree with you on any subject, no matter how mundane, I'm tempted to do so now." She set down her glass on the table with a soft click. "I want to see my son."

Ramirez stood. "Please follow me."

Together they walked over to the riding arena. Two narcos were on duty.

And there, beyond the fence, was a brand-new playset. Paco was hanging upside down from a crossbar. And, when he saw his mother, he produced a yelp of delight. "Mamá!"

Martina hurried to break his fall. They hugged. And both of them cried.

El Cuchillo felt a stab of jealousy. He had millions. But Martina Blanco had something even more precious. He turned and walked away.

La Hacienda Roja, near Agua Frio, Mexico

Serrano was depressed. Three days had passed since his incarceration and subsequent enslavement. Because that's what the prestamistas were: slaves.

And as such they had virtually no freedom of movement. They boarded a truck each morning, and were transported to a location on the Ayo family's sprawling hacienda, where they were assigned to a task involving manual labor. With a jefe there to supervise them, there was almost zero chance to slip away.

And that was the essence of Serrano's plan. Or *had* been his plan because it was in the shitter.

Some of the prisoners picked fruit, and some harvested vegetables, but Serrano was part of the gang that dug drainage ditches. Not the big ones that were maintained with a backhoe, but the "feeders" that ran between rows of trees, and were frequently filled with debris and dirt.

The work wasn't especially difficult, and the trees threw plenty of shade, but it was incredibly boring. So, whenever a member of the Ayo clan came by, it broke the monotony.

Ricardo and Mateo often patrolled together. But on that particular day, Benito was making the rounds. Not in a pickup truck like his brothers, but on a show horse that seemed to prance rather than walk.

And unfortunately, El Niño arrived just as a prestamista named García was urinating against an apple tree. Benito yelled something incomprehensible, spurred his horse, and charged the hapless man. Hooves flailed as the horse reared and García went down.

Then, rather than back off, El Niño urged the animal to attack again. And that was when Serrano lost it. One moment he was standing there, leaning on a shovel, and the next he was in motion. There was no conscious decision. Just the need to stop a murder.

Serrano jumped, got hold of an arm, and dragged Benito down onto the ground. He was vaguely aware of yelling and a commotion, as Ayo family employees converged on the scene and pulled Serrano off of the youth. Then they proceeded to beat the hell out of him.

Eventually someone ordered them to stop, and a half-conscious Serrano was dumped into the back of a pickup. It was half full of decaying fruit, and Serrano was aware of the rotten egg odor as he passed out.

When Serrano awoke, it was from a nightmare and he found himself locked inside a cell. The fact that such a thing existed on a farm spoke to the Ayo main source of income, which was drugs. A business that would inevitably involve locking people up. Informers, policemen, and hostages came to mind. Now it was Serrano's turn.

The plan to infiltrate the farm and kill La Roja had been laughably stupid, and Paco was going to die as a result. It was the lowest moment of Serrano's life.

The hours dragged by. A house maid slid a meager meal through a slot in the steel door. A single ray of sunshine found the narrow window slit and departed as Serrano waited to die.

Then, during what Serrano estimated to be late afternoon, he heard movement. That was followed by the rattle of keys, the sound of a key turning, and a man's voice. "Back away from the door! Place your hands on your head!" Serrano obeyed. He had no other choice.

Two men appeared, both armed with pistols. They cuffed him. Then they escorted him through an underground passageway, up a flight of concrete stairs, and out into bright sunlight.

Serrano blinked, and realized that he'd been held in the Ayo mansion, as he was escorted toward the corrals. Serrano heard cheering, followed by applause, as he was led through a gate. "The rodeo is about to end," one of his escorts said. "Then it'll be your turn."

"My turn to do what?"

"To fight a bull," the other man said. "So, kiss your ass goodbye."

"And now," a male voice said over the P.A. system, "a chance to see justice administered!

"The man you are about to see attacked our Benito, and attempted to kill him. Now you'll have the pleasure of watching One Ton stomp the estúpido to death!"

The announcement provoked applause.

A door opened and Serrano was thrust out into the recently vacated ring. There was stadium seating and at least a hundred spectators.

A narco held a sword up high. Sunlight reflected off the blade. He spoke. "This is the weapon our matador will use to defend himself!" the man announced. "Will he use it skillfully? Or die like the others?"

Serrano was only half listening. All of his senses were heightened. He noticed that the man with the sword was wearing a shoulder holster. The sky was cobalt blue. The odor of horse dung filled his nostrils.

A woman shouted, "¡Atención!" And, as Serrano turned, he could see her. She was wearing a black hat with a flat rim, a red bolero jacket, and standing in front of a high-backed chair.

Was he looking at La Roja? Hell yes, he was! And Benito was seated next to her.

"Behold!" Elena Ayo said. "Justice will be done! Release One Ton."

That was the moment when Serrano accepted the sword, ran the blade through the narco's neck, and jerked it free. Blood began to spurt. Then, as the narco raised both hands to stem the flow, Serrano snatched his Glock.

Did the narco keep one up the spout? Serrano was praying that he did, as he turned and aimed at La Roja. Time seemed to slow as Serrano squeezed the trigger.

Chapter Eleven

La Hacienda Roja, south of Paso del Toro, Mexico

Serrano felt the recoil, and heard the report, as the nine-millimeter slug struck La Roja's chest. The impact threw her back against the throne-like chair. A woman screamed.

Serrano experienced a momentary sense of satisfaction knowing that Paco and Martina would be reunited. Then all hell broke loose.

Visitors hadn't been allowed to bring weapons to the hacienda. But the guards had guns, as did La Roja's sons, and all of them started to fire.

Some of the bullets struck One Ton. None were fatal. But the pain was enough to enrage the beast, which thundered across the arena, determined to kill the only human it could access.

Serrano had two choices: He could run or he could shoot. And Serrano chose option two. A head shot wasn't just preferable, it was absolutely necessary, if Serrano hoped to stop the 2,000-pound bull.

One Ton lowered his head, intent on impaling the human on his horns. Serrano waited until the bull was twenty feet away before he fired. Serrano only had chance to kill the bull before he was impaled. His shot was on target. The bullet struck the top of One Ton's head, killing him.

That didn't stop the thundering mountain of meat, however. Inertia carried the carcass forward. Serrano had to jump to avoid One Ton's potentially lethal horns.

And when Serrano's boots landed on the uneven surface of the bull's back, he lost his balance and nearly fell. *Gotta run… Gotta find a way out… Fifteen bullets left*, Serrano thought, as a bullet snapped past his head. The gate through which One Ton had entered was still open.

Cowboy boots weren't the right footgear, but would have to do, as a guard appeared. He was armed with a black market M27 rifle, which was coming up into position.

Serrano fired, missed, and fired again. The second bullet was low. But it hit a knee. That was better than nothing, and enough to put the narco down.

Serrano shot the narco again, took charge of the Infantry Automatic Rifle, and turned a corner as a hail of bullets struck all around.

The fence consisted of thick planks secured to posts. That meant it was sturdy enough to stop at least some pistol rounds. Serrano stuck the nine down the back of his pants and scuttled along the fence, looking for an opportunity to fight back.

Serrano's chance came when he encountered what seemed like a mountain of hay bales with a roof above. He hurried to climb partway up, found a good spot, and snuggled in. *You have thirty rounds*, Serrano told himself. *Thin them out. And run before they surround you.*

Serrano had been a sniper. And a good one. That, plus the M27's excellent sighting system, meant that he had the upper hand. A narco charged the hay bales. Serrano put him down.

Mateo Ayo appeared with three narcos following behind. Serrano killed them: one, two, three, and four. "Mateo's down!" someone yelled. And that was enough to momentarily stall the attack. *Haul ass,* Serrano thought. *Before reinforcements arrive.*

Serrano left the protection of the bales, made for the sunlight shining beyond, and emerged from the hay barn undetected. But for how long? A small blimp was floating above, looking down on that part of the hacienda.

Serrano eyed it. What was the range anyway? The maximum firing range for an M27 was around 3,900 yards. A bit over two miles. It was worth a try. Serrano raised the rifle, took aim, and fired three shots. Then he ran.

Transpo, Serrano thought. *A car, a motorcycle, anything.*

Serrano was circling the corrals and arena by that time, heading toward the house. That's when he saw two horses. They were tied to a hitching post. Both were saddled.

Serrano knew how to ride, or had known, before he entered the Marine Corps. But that was ten years earlier. He hurried to sling the M27 and mount a horse, which sidestepped. He pulled the animal's head around and kicked its flanks. Would the narcos spot him?

Serrano looked up to see that the mostly deflated surveillance balloon was falling, and would soon hit the ground. That offered a sense of safety which quickly disappeared as a helicopter roared overhead.

Serrano was in among the fruit trees by then, and no more than a flitting shadow, as a narco fired an automatic weapon at him from fifty feet above. The downdraft from the rotors caused leaves to fall and raised a dust cloud. *Get ready,* Serrano told himself. *The flying asshole will need to switch magazines soon.*

Serrano's prophecy came true seconds later. That was his cue to dismount. His horse galloped away. Serrano brought the M27 around and ducked out of the sling.

The helo had turned by then, the gunner was ready, and opened fire. Though protected by a tree trunk, Serrano was woefully conscious of how slender it was, as he waited for the helo to fill his sight. *Aim for the pilot*, Serrano thought. *That's the way to end this.*

The aircraft was coming straight at Serrano, so there was no need to lead it. The canopy appeared, Serrano fired a burst, and had the satisfaction of seeing the machine tilt before crashing, and exploding into flames. A dozen trees caught on fire.

Run, Serrano thought. *Run like your life depends upon it. Cause it sure as hell does.*

Lugar de Paz, Mexico

Martina had gone to work as a way to fill the day and to mask the desperation she felt, but Paco's absence plagued her. As did Nick Serrano's. What if she lost both? As one died in a futile attempt to save the other? Dark thoughts beckoned.

No, Martina told herself. *They're alive. I know they are. And where there's life, there's hope.*

After the final bell rang and her students were gone, Martina cleared her desk and left. There were errands to run. A trip to the grocery store came first. Followed by a visit to La Casa Bonita to pet Macho and feed him.

Then Martina went home, made dinner, and did a load of a laundry. TV was boring. She fell asleep.

When the knock came, it frightened her. Martina stood and paused to grab her assault rifle before standing next to the door. "Who is it?"

The voice was faint. "It's me, Mamá. Let me in."

Martina hurried to turn the lock and open the door. And there, wearing clothes she didn't recognize, was Paco. "¡Madre de Dios! It's you! It's really you!"

They hugged and Martina cried. Paco tried to comfort her. "It's okay, I'm fine."

Martina looked for a vehicle but didn't see one. So, she brought her boy inside, checked for injuries, and couldn't find any. "Are you hungry?" Paco nodded.

Even though Martina's heart was full, she continued to worry.

La Roja was dead. Paco's presence was proof of that. Did Ramirez have a spy inside the Ayo family compound? Otherwise, how else would El Cuchillo know?

But what about Nick? Was he alive? Martina prayed that he was.

Near Agua Frio, Mexico

Once the sun went down, it was cold. But Serrano had been able to rip three holes in an Ayo farm burlap bag, which he wore like a poncho. That helped some, but it was still chilly.

The good news was that he was free, possessed two weapons, and one of the surveillance balloons was down. The bad news was that the narcos were patrolling the hacienda in trucks, on dirt bikes, and horses. So how to escape?

Serrano had graduated from the Marine Corps' Survival, Evasion, Resistance and Escape school. One of the instructors liked to talk about opportunities. "You may not have a plan," he liked to say. "But you'll have opportunities. The challenge is to recognize them for what they are."

So, Serrano thought. *What are my opportunities?* He couldn't think of any. That left him with his only option—to travel west, toward the highway which bordered the farm. Once across the ribbon of concrete, Serrano hoped the danger level would decrease.

But, when he arrived at the western edge of the apple orchard, Serrano discovered that narco vehicles were passing so frequently that it would be risky to cross. Especially given the open areas on both sides of the highway.

However, thanks to time spent digging drainage ditches, Serrano knew that a large culvert ran under the road. Was that the opportunity he was looking for? Perhaps so.

Serrano remained in among the trees until he came to a major ditch. An ankle-deep flow of water was running west, and as a motorcycle approached, Serrano had to elbow his way forward.

Cold water soaked the burlap bag and the front of his pants. But it couldn't be helped. The M27 was resting across his arms while he elbowed his way forward.

Serrano heard the growl of an engine, as he belly-crawled into the culvert. The inside diameter was large enough to accommodate him, although the top of his head scraped concrete at times. *At least I don't have to worry about snakes*, Serrano thought. *They aren't likely to linger in moving water.*

Eventually, after what seemed like an eternity, Serrano emerged from the west end of the culvert. He could see a scattering of lights up ahead.

After finding his way up and out of the ditch, Serrano dashed from shadow to shadow before arriving in what appeared to be a barrio pobre.

From what Serrano could see the homes were small, frequently constructed using found materials, and almost always surrounded by piles of junk. Old cars lurked in the shadows, a man was shouting at someone, and pop music leaked out of a decrepit camp trailer.

Who were the people living there? Serrano wondered. Narcos? And their families? That was likely. The Ayo family's foot soldiers had to sleep somewhere.

A dog barked and jerked on its chain as Serrano passed a shack. But no one came out to investigate. *An opportunity*,

Serrano thought. *I need another opportunity.*

Headlights swept across a graffiti-covered freight container which, judging from the collection of children's toys scattered about, was somebody's home. And there, leaning against the container, was a dirt bike! Was it operable? What about fuel?

Serrano dashed from one shadow to another, took a look around, and sidled up to the bike. He could be spotted at any time. So, rather than inspect his prize then and there, Serrano chose to grab the motorcycle's handlebars and walk it away.

The fact that he could suggested that the steering lock was off, or had been disabled. Did that mean the bike had been stolen? Serrano hoped so.

Once in the shadows, Serrano felt for an ignition key and was pleased to find one. And, by sticking a dry twig down into the tank, he confirmed that there was at least some gas in it.

Footpaths branched every which way. Serrano followed one that looked like it would intersect the highway, soon learned that it didn't, and had to start over again. But eventually, after two misses, he scored.

A dirt track led out of the scrub and down an incline to the highway. Could Serrano pose as a searcher? He thought so. The long gun would reinforce that assumption.

So, Serrano swung a leg over the seat, checked to ensure that the motorcycle was in neutral, and turned the key. The engine sputtered and died. He tried again. Success! The motor chattering loudly, Serrano engaged the clutch and shifted into first gear. A blob of light led the way.

Serrano didn't have his phone so he couldn't summon a ride. And since the dirt bike's top speed was 30mph, it had to ride on the shoulder, which was dangerous. Never mind the fact that he would run out of gas long before he arrived in Lugar de Paz.

That forced Serrano to take a side trip to Valle de Oro and Father Olmo, where he put in a call to Father Colon and confirmed that Paco was free. He felt a huge sense of relief.

Serrano was then free to shower, have his sutures removed, and don the clothes Father Olmo provided. Next, after a hearty breakfast, Serrano lay down on Olmo's guest cot and went to sleep. And that's where he was, in a world free of conflict, when something soft brushed his cheek. Serrano opened his eyes to find that Martina was looking down at him. She kissed him again. "I'm so glad that you survived, mi amor."

Serrano smiled. "You took a day off from school."

"It's Saturday," Martina replied pragmatically. "Paco is with Carmen… And can't wait to see you."

Serrano swung his feet over onto the floor. "The feeling is mutual. He's a good boy," Serrano added, while he stood up. "And he'll grow up to be a good man."

"Thanks to you," Martina said, as she looked up at him. They kissed.

The drive to Lugar de Paz was spent talking. Martina wanted to know everything there was to know about the assassination, and when Serrano described La Roja's death, she cried. "God guided your bullet… There's no other explanation."

Serrano didn't think so. If God took sides, there wouldn't be any evil in the world. But he kept that opinion to himself.

Later that evening, when Paco was asleep, they snuggled in bed. "So," Martina said, after they made love. "What's next for you? Gardening?"

Serrano laughed. "I had lots of time to think while I was digging ditches, and decided that I need to visit the United States."

Martina stared at him. "Why?"

"Because," Serrano replied, "I thought Mr. Yankovic would

get tired of sending people to kill me and give up. But I was wrong. And it's only a matter of time before Yankovic's thugs hurt people here in Lugar de Paz while trying to cap me. And the Ayo family might come looking for me as well."

Serrano had been honest with Martina all along about Yankovic and the theft. "*No*," she said emphatically. "The people of Luga de Paz owe you! We'll defend you."

Serrano kissed her. "I know you mean that. But what about Paco? And his classmates? Any one of them could get killed during a gun battle."

It was, Serrano knew, the right argument for the right person. After all, Martina was both a teacher and a mother. Tears began to flow. "When will the waiting stop?" Martina demanded. "Please. Please make it stop."

"I will," Serrano promised. "And then I'll plant some flowers."

Chapter Twelve

San Antonio, Texas

The airport nearest to Lugar de Paz was in Torreón, which had plenty of flights to San Antonio. Serrano was seated just aft of the starboard wing in the window seat, where he could see the scenery pass below.

But Serrano's thoughts were mainly focused on the mission ahead. His first task was to locate his ex-wife, and find out if she still had some of his belongings. Mementoes mostly, photos taken while in the Corps, and other odds and ends.

Then Serrano planned to dig up intel on Mr. Yankovic. He was tempted to contact Cory Dalton—the guy responsible for hooking him up with Yankovic—and try to obtain some info that way. But, linking Dalton to Yankovic's death would be a shit-assed thing to do.

Plus, even though the two of them had been tight in the Marine Corps, there was the possibility that Dalton would rat him out. Some people change over time.

Serrano's thoughts were interrupted by the usual pre-landing blah-blah. The plane touched down shortly afterwards. There was a fifteen-minute wait before they reached the gate.

After waiting for passengers in the forward part of the plane to file out, Serrano removed his knapsack from the overhead bin, and followed along behind them.

The jet bridge led to the terminal which, like most terminals, was very busy. The crowd swirled, and Serrano was about to head for baggage claim when two men grabbed his arms. One flashed a badge. "Nick Serrano?"

"Yes. What's going on?"

"We're placing you under arrest for the murders of your ex-wife Valerie Carter, and her companion, Cody Carl. You have the right to remain silent. Anything you say can, and will, be used against you in a court of law. And, you have a right to an attorney."

The second officer gave Serrano a pat down as the first detective spoke. Serrano felt a sense of shock. "Valerie's dead? Cody Carl? Who's he?"

"Save the innocent act for Judge McHenry," the policeman said, as Serrano's wrists were handcuffed behind him. "Did you check any luggage?"

"Yes, one suitcase."

"Okay, let's get it."

Serrano's mind raced as he was escorted through the terminal to baggage claim. Who killed Valerie and why? And who was this Cody person? A boyfriend? Maybe he was the actual target, and Val was collateral damage.

Then another possibility occurred to him. What about the three men who invaded his house shortly after his arrival in Lugar de Paz? The blabbermouth was named Creedy according to the ID in his wallet. And made no bones about working for Yankovic.

At the time Serrano wondered how the hitmen managed to find him. Now he knew. She told them, probably under duress, and they killed her. And Cody Carl too.

Serrano felt a deep sense of remorse. If his theory was correct, he shared responsibility for Valerie's death. Something she didn't deserve. But Yankovic did. And the bastard was going to pay.

"Here it is," the second officer said, as he emerged from the crowd. "Are you going to give me the combo? Or will we have to pry it open?"

Serrano shrugged. "3-2-1."

"Wow!" the first officer said. "What a fucking genius. No one would ever figure that out."

"I don't have anything to hide," Serrano replied.

"Not even the pistols in the suitcase?" the second policeman inquired.

Serrano had the regulation memorized. "A passenger can transport unloaded firearms in a locked, hard-sided container as checked luggage, so long as they declare the firearm and/or ammunition to the airline when checking their bag," Serrano told them. "And I did so. I have the paperwork to prove it."

"I'm glad to hear the murder weapon or weapons were properly processed," officer one said. "Come on, Mack... Let's book this clown."

The trip from the airport to the Magistrate of Bexar County's office near Cattleman Square took 20 minutes. Initial processing lasted the better part of two hours, which Serrano spent in a small locked room.

Then a gray-haired woman dressed in a running outfit and carrying a briefcase arrived. "Hi! I'm Jennifer Garvey, your court appointed attorney. Sorry about the wait. They always call me when ex-Marines are charged, and I was on the other side of town."

Serrano stood to shake her hand. It was cool and firm. "Why's that? Was your father a Marine?"

Garvey pushed a sleeve up. And there it was, an Eagle, Globe and Anchor tattoo. "Semper fi."

Serrano's eyes widened. "You were a Marine?"

"You betcha," Garvey replied. "More specifically, a Marine Judge Advocate. I'm retired now, but I have a soft spot for jarheads."

"So," Garvey said, as she sat down. "You're accused of a double homicide. I'm your public defender. Whatever you tell me is covered by attorney-client privilege. Let's start with the obvious question. Did you do it?"

"No," Serrano answered. "I didn't."

Garvey eyed him cynically. "Can you prove that?"

"I think so," Serrano said. "When was my ex-wife murdered?"

Garvey told him.

Serrano nodded. "I was in Mexico on that day. And the stamp on my passport will prove it."

Garvey eyed a sheet of paper. "That's helpful, but insufficient. According to this document the police believe that you entered Mexico to establish an alibi, came back across the border without passing through customs, and committed two murders. Then you recrossed the border into Mexico illegally. So, according to them, you had an opportunity. As for motive, Valerie's mother claims you were very angry when her daughter left you for another man. Especially since she spent your savings on him."

"Multiple witnesses will corroborate that I was in the village of Lugar de Paz that day," Serrano told her. "As for being angry, I was. But that doesn't mean I would hurt Valerie."

"That's a good start," Garvey agreed. "However, according to the Mayor of Lugar de Paz, you shot numerous people there."

Suddenly Serrano understood how the detectives knew he was traveling to San Antonio. Mayor Aguilar tipped them off. Another score to settle.

"I was forced to defend myself," Serrano replied. "But, the Federales investigated and cleared me. Their reports will confirm that."

"I'll follow up on that," Garvey promised. "How do you explain what the police are calling the 'possible murder weapons' found in your luggage?"

"I followed all of the procedures for carrying weapons on a plane," Serrano assured her. "And I have the paperwork to prove it. Plus, as a person with dual citizenship, I have the right to carry concealed weapons in Texas."

"That's true," Garvey agreed, as she scribbled a note to herself.

"Now, one last thing. Why did you have twenty-thousand dollars in your suitcase?"

"I was hoping to buy a used truck and drive it back to Lugar de Paz," Serrano lied.

Garvey looked skeptical. "A truck? Okay. But regardless of your intentions, you'll need to post a bond. So, the money will come in handy." Garvey made another note. "Here's the deal. By now an assistant district attorney has examined the police report, and based on their allegations, will probably accept the case. I'll meet you in court, where I'll try to counter the evidence submitted thus far. As part of that effort, I will request that they compare slugs from your weapons to the bullets found in the dead bodies. Then," Garvey added, "assuming the witnesses in Mexico confirm your story, you'll be off the hook. A policeman will arrive shortly to escort you to the courtroom." She rose and collected her things. "Oh, and one more thing… Keep your mouth shut. I'll do the talking."

The hearing went exactly as Garvey said it would. And Serrano's bond was set at $50,000. Serrano had to pay the bondsman $5,000.

The prosecuting attorney objected and suggested that Serrano was a flight risk given his dual citizenship.

But the judge disagreed, citing the stamps in Serrano's passports, and the likelihood that witnesses would attest to his presence in Mexico on the day the murders were committed. He also mentioned Serrano's spotless record in the Marine Corps, including the Silver Star awarded to him in Syria. Both of which had been put forward by Garvey—much to Serrano's surprise.

"I still have some connections," Garvey told him after the hearing. "And they come in handy. Come on, let's get your bond. We can take care of it online if you have a credit card."

Serrano had a card. So, he was free to leave shortly thereafter, and promised to stay in touch regarding the outcome of the initial investigation.

It was early evening by then. After renting the cheapest car he could find, Serrano checked into a budget hotel and had dinner at the McDonald's next door.

The five grand, nonrefundable payment to the bail bondsman had taken a big chunk out of his working capital, so it was important to keep costs down.

Rather than phone Martina, and worry her with the news that he'd been arrested, Serrano sent her a cheerful text message indicating that he was safe and would stay in touch.

Then it was time to make his bed on the floor, sans even one pistol, since the police had them and were going to conduct tests. That meant Serrano would be SOL if a hitman broke in. But there was nothing he could do about it. Not yet anyway.

Sleep came quickly. And, when morning arrived Serrano felt pretty good after consuming a breakfast sandwich and a grande Pike.

It would have been nice to call Valerie's mom, both to pay

his respects and to find out where Val was buried. But Serrano was under orders to stay away from his ex-mother-in-law lest he be accused of tampering with a witness.

So, Serrano used Papá's laptop to go online. And when he googled Valerie's name, Serrano found articles about both the murders and the funerals.

A detective was quoted as saying that the murders were consistent with mob style executions. He also said that authorities were interested in talking to Valerie Carter's ex-husband, a man with dual citizenship, who might or might not be in Mexico.

And, thanks to coverage of the funerals, Serrano knew that Val was buried in the suburb where her mother lived.

During the drive to the cemetery Serrano was deluged with memories both good and bad. There was the incredible high of falling in love, the joy of meeting up in Spain, and the nonstop sex.

But there was also the sadness that followed a month without calls, texts, or letters. And the surge of anger, when Valerie confirmed what Serrano already suspected, that there was someone else.

The fact that Val had spent Serrano's savings didn't come to light until the divorce. And with it the most hurtful thing she'd ever said to him. "I didn't steal your money... I earned it."

So, why visit Valerie's grave? To dance on it? No. In spite of the pain, a part of him still loved her. And, regardless of what Serrano felt, his ex-wife didn't deserve to be murdered.

After finding the cemetery, and with guidance from a maintenance worker, Serrano found the plot. Valerie's maiden name was inscribed on the headstone and flanked by cherubs—which she would have detested.

Serrano knelt. *Hey Val, it's me, Nick. I'm not very good with words. You know that. But I want to tell you how sorry I am,*

especially since your death was ultimately my fault, even if I didn't
pull the trigger. I wish I could go back and fix it. But I can't.

I'm not likely to go to heaven, so I won't see you there, but rest
assured... The other man who is responsible for your death will be
with me in hell. And with that, Serrano placed a single rose on
the headstone. Then he stood and walked away.

After buying lunch at a Taco Time, Serrano returned to his
hotel room, and went to work.

The search term "Maurice Yankovic" turned up a surprising
number of hits. And a surprising number of identities: There
was Yankovic the bitcoin trader. Yankovic the off-road racer.
And Yankovic the philanthropist. But Serrano found no mention of Yankovic the mob chief or Yankovic the killer.

And there was something else too. Something that might
or might not be significant, and that was Yankovic's new crib.
The old-new castle was the subject of a detailed feature story in
Colorado Magazine.

The home, called The Eagle's Nest, had been constructed
by a timber baron named Oliver West, originally Oliver Lieb-
knecht, who built the castle as a labor of love. And according to
legend, spent one-million 1932 dollars to complete it. A great
deal of which was spent on the serpentine access road which,
according to the breathless reporter, "...crept up between lofty
peaks to claim a piece of the sky."

It was by necessity a two-season residence due to landslides
and heavy snows.

But when the Nest was accessible, it was a retreat for not
only West, but luminaries like the governor of Colorado, the
nature photographer John Freed, and a steady trickle of Holly-
wood celebrities.

Sadly, West died of a heart attack in his sixties, causing the
castle to be sold to the first of more than a dozen owners, all of

whom were infatuated with the home's spectacular views.

But eventually the cost of maintenance, or some sort of misfortune, got the better of each. After all, it was a rare individual who could afford a getaway that had to be staffed year-round, but could only be accessed for three to four months at a time.

That was until a fantastically wealthy businesswoman named Esther Bruck purchased the Eagle's Nest for a measly two million, remodeled it from top to bottom—and most important of all—installed a helicopter landing pad. An amenity that theoretically made the place accessible year-round, although the article was careful to say, "Weather is a factor. And there are days, even weeks, when the castle is cut off from the rest of the world."

And that's how things were until Bruck was diagnosed with cancer and put the Nest on the market yet again. But this time it was a new type of "king" who claimed the home, a bitcoin magnate named Maurice Yankovic, who made no bones about his need for a doomsday residence. A place where he would purportedly be safe from a nuclear war, a catastrophic meteor hit, or civil unrest.

Serrano sat and stared at a photo of the home. It consisted of a square tower with a crenelated top, two diagonally opposed towers with pitched roofs, a central fortification with high arched windows, a partial moat, and what was said to be a functioning drawbridge. All in keeping with West's original fantasy.

Various thoughts flitted through Serrano's mind. *The sale had closed while he was in Mexico. What's really going on?* Maybe Yankovic *was* worried by the possibilities outlined in the article. Or, maybe he, Yankovic, had enemies. People who wanted to seize control of his lucrative crypto scam.

But there's another possibility, Serrano thought. *What if he's afraid of me? The guy he hasn't been able to kill, the guy who might come for him in real life, and not just his dreams.*

Two days passed before Serrano's phone chirped and Garvey delivered the good news. Father Colon, Martina Blanco, and Carlos Alonso had all verified his presence in Lugar de Paz on the day of Valerie's murder.

Furthermore, the forensics tests had come back negative, and there were no traces of Serrano's DNA at the crime scene. As for the final formalities, Garvey volunteered to take care of those, and would take custody of his pistols. And, since Serrano was unemployed, the county would pay her fee.

Serrano thanked Garvey and promised to retrieve the weapons prior to departing for Mexico. Because, now that forensic tests had been performed on the pistols, the last thing he wanted to do was use either one of them during the showdown with Mr. Yankovic.

Preparatory work began. The first step was to get the tail number of the helicopter that Yankovic used to travel to and from the Eagle's Nest. And, since all flights were a matter of public record, that data was available.

It took hours of sorting, but eventually Serrano discovered that a helicopter belonging to Trenton Aviation in Nickle City, Colorado, made regular trips to the Eagle's Nest. Moreover, those flights coincided with the arrival and departures of a private jet registered to the Yankovic Corporation.

That was the good news. The bad news was that Yankovic's trips were totally random. As a result, there was no way to know when the piece of shit might visit his castle. A reality that Serrano would have to take into account when devising a plan.

His first challenge was to reach the area where the aerie was located without leaving a paper trail. And the best way to do that was to drive, pay cash for everything, and camp out along the way.

For $9,970, Serrano was able to buy a 2011 Chevrolet Silverado with a crew cab. The purchase was consistent with what Serrano had told Garvey.

Then, after turning his phone off, Serrano set out on the thousand-mile trip, stopping occasionally to purchase items on his shopping list.

Weapons came first because Serrano wanted to acquire them in Texas, which didn't require records or background checks. Camping gear was gradually purchased in cities along his route and put to use in public campgrounds, where he slept in the bed of the truck with the canopy to protect him from rain.

By the time Serrano arrived in the vicinity of Yankovic's getaway, he was ready to tackle his mission. The final night of the trip was spent in the Double Nickle RV Park, where he paid for a week in advance, before leaving on a "backpacking trip."

A twenty-mile hike lay ahead at that point, and Serrano was carrying about one hundred pounds of gear, similar to the loadouts he carried during combat missions. But that was then. And now, years later, the load felt like twice that amount as Serrano followed a series of twisting-turning trails toward his destination.

Serrano's headlamp was on and he held his new Smith & Wesson .357 in his hand as he hiked. Was an animal attack likely? No, but anything was possible.

It soon became apparent that Serrano's fantasy of hiking twenty miles before dawn was just that, a fantasy. His back hurt, his legs hurt, and his hurts hurt.

So, after ten miles Serrano used his Jetboil to prepare a dehydrated meal, drank cold water from a stream, and deployed the bivvy-sleeping bag combo—which had proven itself during the trip to Nickel.

The night passed uneventfully. Serrano tackled the last ten miles after a hearty breakfast. It was a mostly uphill trek that ended near the base of the pinnacle upon which the Eagle's Nest rested.

As Serrano looked up, he saw gray rock, snowy ledges, and hints of green where hardy shrubs had managed to eke out a living. *Tomorrow*, Serrano thought. *Win or lose.*

Chapter Thirteen

Near Nickel, Colorado

The Corkscrew. That's what industrialist Oliver West called the narrow path that started at the Eagle's Nest and circled the underlying pinnacle of rock all the way down to the ground.

The trail was, according to the plans drawn up by architect Homer Williams, a route that he likened to a fire escape. As such, it would serve as a way to evacuate the castle in case the structure caught fire and the road was closed.

Though referred to in the early plans, the Corkscrew never came up again until it was mentioned in an article which appeared in an architectural magazine in 1958. "The path isn't for the faint of heart," the journalist wrote. "But it would offer a means of escape in an emergency."

Was the Corkscrew maintained? And if so, was it guarded? Serrano was about to find out.

The sun was starting to rise as Serrano circled the rock formation, looking for the point where the trail began, or ended, depending on one's point of view.

The trail's endpoint was on the southside—he knew that. And sure enough, after fifteen minutes of searching, Serrano found two posts and a rusty chain. The sign that dangled from it read *No Trespassing* and was perforated with bullet holes.

Thus encouraged, Serrano eased his way around a post, then paused to adjust his pack, before beginning what promised to be a difficult climb. One foot in front of the other. *That's the secret,* Serrano thought. And it was, at first.

There had been a hand rope in the old days, secured to railroad spikes that were driven into crevices every fifty feet or so. But that amenity had rotted away and never been replaced. Question one had been answered: No, the Corkscrew wasn't maintained. There was no need. Not with helicopters to call on.

But an hour in and a couple of hundred feet up the narrow trail, Serrano came to a washout. A place where a section of the path had been carried away by the runoff from successive storms, leaving nothing more than a narrow ledge to stand on.

There were some hardy-looking shrubs however. And, by grabbing onto them, Serrano thought he might be able to edge along the six-foot-wide gap.

So, with arms raised, and his face pressed against cold granite, Serrano began to toe his way across. And that worked reasonably well for a while.

Then Serrano came to a spot where he had to lunge for the next handhold, risking everything. He managed to grab a juniper, then another, and another.

By side-slipping along, Serrano was able to regain the trail. He chose to pause at that point and celebrate by eating a trail bar. Miserly sips of water were used to wash it down. What would Serrano find up top? A ready source of water? Or a heavily guarded summit, with no access to water? He feared the latter.

Now, as Serrano edged along the east side of the rockface, he could see the ribbon of road that was still used to bring supplies up to the nest. Was it patrolled? And if so, would someone notice the tiny stick figure high above them? All he could do was hope for the best.

As Serrano rounded a curve, he was forced to stop in front of an eight-foot gap. Six rusty rods protruded from the cliff face. And, judging from the weather-worn plank that rested on them, they had been part of a bridge at one time.

What to do? The plank might or might not bear his weight. Serrano considered trying to heave his pack across the gap, but decided that it was too heavy, and would probably fall to the ground hundreds of feet below.

That left him no choice but to "walk" on the rods while hugging the cliff face, where he could use his right hand to help maintain his balance. It was the most demanding crossing Serrano had faced. And he was scared.

There were two ways for Serrano to proceed: he could run, or he could walk. Serrano chose to run in order to lighten the load on any one rod and generate the impetus required to carry him across.

With that in mind Serrano backed away, eyed the rods, and threw himself forward. The first rod was solid. But the second gave way, and threatened to dump Serrano into the abyss below, as he jumped to the third. It held. As did the fourth. And that enabled Serrano to reach solid ground.

That's where Serrano fell to his knees, heart pounding, and body trembling. He rolled to one side, so that the pack wasn't pressing down on him, and closed his eyes.

A full ten minutes passed before Serrano lurched to his feet. He was tired. Dog tired. And worried that he might be exhausted by the time he arrived.

But there wasn't enough room to camp, so Serrano forced himself to continue walking. And, fifteen minutes later, he spotted a radio antenna.

It was vitally important to conceal his identity. So, Serrano paused to pull a three-hole ski mask on, along with a pair of latex gloves.

Before creeping ahead, Serrano checked his weapons, which consisted of the .357 and a Ruger Mark IV .22 pistol. Was Yankovic in residence? There was no way to be certain, so Serrano had to assume that he was.

Instead of barging into the castle immediately, Serrano wanted to gather as much intel as he could. And, to accomplish that, he needed to find a good hide. A spot where he could observe without being noticed.

Serrano knew from his days as a sniper that it was important to go low, and go slow, no matter how uncomfortable it might be. That meant dropping to the ground and elbowing his way forward.

Once Serrano had a clear view of the radio antenna, he made use of a pocket monocular to check the tower for cameras. He didn't see any. There was a bright orange windsock for the helicopter pilots though, plus a weather module that would provide Yankovic and his minions with data regarding wind speed and temperature.

Part of the castle was visible to the right, and that was where Yankovic was likely to be. So, Serrano belly crawled in that direction.

From the top of the rise, with a wind-sculptured bush for cover, Serrano could see the helipad. It appeared to be in good condition, and was marked with a huge "H," surrounded by a red circle. The fact that it was empty didn't mean much.

Perhaps Yankovic was inside, relaxing in front of a fire. That would account for the smoke coming out of the Nest's chimney. Or, maybe the staff was enjoying the castle's amenities while their boss was away. Anything was possible.

Serrano was careful to quarter his surroundings with his monocular. And sure enough, there were two sentry stations, both made of concrete and topped with peaked roofs. Plus, there could be more in areas he couldn't see.

And that raised an interesting question. Where did the castle's electricity come from?

The answer was the banks of motorized solar panels off to Serrano's right. A rise blocked most of the view, but one end of the installation was visible. And, a person hiding under the panels would not only be invisible from above, but would have an unobstructed view of the inner courtyard.

The sun was low in the sky by then, the wind was picking up, and the temperature was dropping. Serrano was starting to shiver by the time he crawled in under the solar panels.

By collecting loose rocks, he was able to fashion a low wall which screened him from the castle, and provided a flat spot to lie upon.

The next task was to deploy the bivvy-sleeping bag combo and slide inside. Serrano felt warmer within minutes. Unfortunately, he had to use some of his precious water to prepare a dehydrated meal. But he was hungry, and it was important to keep his strength up.

Then it was time to zip himself in, close his eyes, and sleep. He thought it would be difficult. It wasn't.

Serrano awoke to the sound of rain drops pattering on the solar panel above him. It was dark, but he forced himself to leave the comfort of the bags and crawl to the point where he could hold his water bottle under the runoff from a panel. It was cold. And it seemed to take forever to fill the canteen. But finally, when the task was complete, Serrano went back to his hideaway.

Warmth returned, as did sleep, followed by the start of a

brand-new day. Serrano prepared some instant hot chocolate and ate a trail bar.

Maybe the bastard is in there, Serrano thought. *I'll watch. I'll wait. And, if necessary, I'll enter tonight.*

Time seemed to stretch. Clouds crawled across the sky. The sentries were relieved. That suggested six men working three shifts, and possibly more, since he couldn't see the entire complex.

Night fell. Lights appeared and disappeared. The sentries were relieved again. Who were they on the lookout for anyway? *People like me,* Serrano decided.

Then, just as Serrano was about to eat a candy bar, the lights around the helipad came on. *He's coming!* Serrano concluded. *And about to receive guests. One of whom will be me.*

The helicopter nav lights appeared, and it made a terrible racket while it circled prior to landing. Pole-mounted lights lit the pad as three figures got out, one of whom shoved another, whose wrists were secured behind them. A prisoner!

Good, Serrano thought. *The focus will be on them.*

Was one of the other passengers Yankovic? He couldn't tell.

The logical thing was to use the suppressed .22 to kill the sentries. But Serrano couldn't bring himself to murder them in cold blood. Instead, under the cover of darkness, he chose to make his way to the castle, find a way in, and hope for the best.

Serrano couldn't leave the pack behind. It, and the contents within, were layered with his fingerprints and DNA and would reveal his identity.

Reaching the castle was a time-consuming process. The first task was to identify an intermediate objective. The second was to scurry over to it and look around. Then it was necessary to start over again.

Once Serrano was on the walkway that ran along the back

of the castle, he saw a light leaking out of a mostly closed door. To the kitchen? Yes, judging from the strong smell of curry, and the whir of a fan.

He sidled up to the door and peeked inside. A man was standing in front of a range frying something. Serrano slid inside, hoping to pistol whip the domestic and immobilize him. It didn't work.

The cook reached for a cleaver and Serrano shot him. Though not a fan of semiautomatic pistols, Serrano had to admit that the purpose-built Ruger was ideal for the job.

The suppressed pistol produced nothing more than a gentle clack as the .22 slug struck the target's forehead. The cook slumped to the floor and the cleaver clattered. Serrano waited for a response. There was none.

Serrano paused to turn the range off before proceeding into a shadowy hallway. And from there into a large dining room. Rather than the luxurious interior that he had imagined, boxes were stacked along one wall and the furniture was covered with sheets.

Serrano could hear voices from beyond the dining room. "It's very simple," a man said. "Either you tell me what I want to know, or my men will gang rape you until you do."

Was that Yankovic's voice? Yes, judging from the content, it was.

But who was the woman Yankovic was threatening? Suddenly, rather than the simple hit that Serrano had envisioned, he was ass deep in something complicated.

Both pistols were up and ready as Serrano eased his way into the sitting area which opened onto a large living room. And that's where the half-naked woman was, tied to an ornate chair. Yankovic slapped her. "Speak up, bitch... What's it going to be?"

The woman licked her swollen lips. "I'll take the gangbang. Let's get on with it."

Three men were visible. Serrano shot the one on the left with the .357, and the one on the right with the .22, killing both. Yankovic whirled to face Serrano. "Who the hell are *you*?"

"The person who's going to kill you," Serrano replied. "Pull if you want to. It won't make any difference."

Light flashed off chrome as Yankovic attempted to draw his sidearm. Two bullets hit him. One in the head and one in the chest. The body produced a thump as it hit the floor.

"Behind you!" the woman warned.

Serrano turned as a guard fired. The bullet passed within an inch of Serrano's head and shattered a mirror in the room.

Serrano's aim was a hair off and hit the assailant's shoulder rather than his chest. The man staggered, tried to remain upright, and fell as a .357 round ripped through his throat.

Chances were that the guard was from outside, and Serrano knew there were more, so he hurried to free the woman. "Who are you?"

"You can call me Harper," she replied. "Hand me that jacket. It's cold in here. Are there more of them?"

"Yes."

"Okay," the woman said, as she hurried to retrieve a nine. "Let's shoot our way out of here."

Serrano watched the professional manner in which Harper ejected the pistol's magazine, checked to see how many cartridges remained, and reinserted it. "Law enforcement?"

Harper nodded. "And you?"

"A man with a grudge."

"Okay," she said. "Remind me not to piss you off. Let's go."

The pack was a weighty encumbrance. But Serrano couldn't shed it and didn't. His plan, such as it was, entailed finding a vehicle and driving out. So, he led Harper to the front door, pushed it open, and waited for a reaction. There wasn't any.

Stairs led to the drawbridge, which was in the down position. An automatic weapon chattered. Bullets dug divots in the wood as Harper fired at the muzzle flashes. The weapon fell silent.

Serrano waved her forward, then followed a path to stairs, and down to the parking area. A pole-mounted light shone down onto two vehicles. One started with a roar. Serrano could see a silhouette through the rear window so he fired. The driver slumped forward.

"Good work," Harper said. "I'll drive. You shoot."

Harper opened the driver's side door, pulled the corpse out, and let it fall to the pavement.

Serrano paused long enough to shoot at the tires on the other vehicle, before throwing the pack into the back seat. Once inside the SUV, he hurried to strap in and reload.

"So," Serrano said. "What did Mr. Yankovic do to deserve you attention?"

"Drugs," Harper replied. "Among other things."

Serrano remembered the boxes stacked inside the castle. Yankovic had been using the Eagle's Nest as a very difficult-to-access warehouse rather than a vacation home. Well, not anymore.

"How did you get up there?" Harper inquired, as they rounded another curve.

"There's an old trail on the other side of the peak," Serrano replied. "I walked up."

Harper glanced in his direction. "You're not going to give me a name, are you?"

"Nope. How 'bout you? Or is Harper all I'm going to get?"

"That's right," Harper replied. "I'm working undercover."

They laughed.

"Listen, Grudge," Harper said. "One of Yankovic's competitors knows about the Eagle's Nest. They may or may not be coming up this road. Assuming they are, it's gonna get real hairy."

Serrano reached back to grab the submachinegun he'd seen on the back seat. He put it between them. "This is for you. Your nine will run out of ammo in no time."

"Damn," Harper replied. "I'm in love. Are you available?"

"No, but thanks for asking."

"Can she shoot?"

"Yes, she can."

"Then I'm happy for you," Harper said. "I see headlights. Three sets. I plan to push the first vehicle into the second without triggering the airbags. We'll improvise after that."

"Make it happen," Serrano replied, as they swerved onto a short stretch of straightaway.

Harper's reply was lost as the vehicles collided. The SUV was bigger than the sedan and shoved it back. Serrano was thrown against his harness. Metal screeched, the windshield shattered, and the hood popped up.

Harper threw herself out and Serrano did likewise. He saw muzzle flashes, fired at them, and a man fell.

Harper fired three-round bursts as she came level with the sedan's passenger side. A man was waving a pistol and trying to release his harness at the same time. The last thing he saw were flashes of light.

Serrano was on the ground, elbowing his way forward when he came face-to-face with a man headed in the other direction. He was encumbered with an SMG. Serrano wasn't. He fired both pistols. One missed and one didn't.

Silence settled over the scene. "Grudge?" Harper inquired.

"Are you okay?"

"Never better," Serrano said, as he stood. "And you?"

"My face hurts," Harper replied. "And I'll bet it looks like raw hamburger. But some lipstick will fix that. Our limo awaits. I'll drop you off, find a phone, and call for the cavalry. Does that sound good?"

"Yes, it does," Serrano lied, as he returned to the SUV.

"Grudge?" Harper inquired as she arrived next to car three. "Where are you?"

There was no answer. Just the slam of a door, and the rattle of rocks, as Serrano made his way downslope.

Chapter Fourteen

In the Sierra Madre Oriental Mountains

The Sierra Madre Oriental Mountains ran from a point near the Rio Grande River south to Mexico City and were made up of limestone and shale.

Some of the Sierra Madre Oriental peaks rose to more than 12,000 feet, and were part of the 4,000-mile-long American Cordillera, or backbone, that ran the length of North, Central, and South America.

All of which was lost on Captain García and the men of army Unit 777. A special forces outfit made famous by its run-ins with Las Patriotas, and the by the way it had been able to disrupt the flow of narcotics out west.

Now, as García led his men up a narrow trail, the late afternoon sun threw long shadows across the ground, and the thin air made it difficult to breathe. Other tracks branched to the left and right making it difficult to navigate as well.

How did the narcos do it? They had guides. Men and women who'd had been born in remote mountain villages, and like fleas on a dog, fed off the cartels.

As for the cartel leaders, they came and went in planes small enough to land on dirt runways, few of which were known to the authorities.

And that's where Unit 777 was headed. To a godforsaken strip called El Jorobado, thus named due to a hump halfway down the runway.

The site was, according to an informer, going to be the location of a massive transaction involving a ton of "product," and bales of American currency. And García planned to capture both.

Major García had a ring to it, and his parents would be proud. The thought put some pep in his step as he the thumbed the radio. "¡Apurase!"

The pace quickened as the company of one hundred two soldiers followed their commanding officer through a confluence of trails, across a fast-moving stream, and toward a path that zigzagged up a steep slope. Scouts preceded the rest of the soldiers and had disappeared around a bend. Would they come under fire? Quite possibly. And García's nerves were wired tight.

But, when the report came in, it was unexpectedly positive. "The area is clear. Over."

García was able to confirm that when he rounded a bend and entered an open area. A tattered wind sock drooped from a rough-hewn pole, and the runway called El Jorobado was there before him. The strip ran north and south, and was flanked by rocks, raggedy tents and drifts of windblown trash.

García saw those things, but his attention was centered on something else. And that was the man nailed to a cross. Not just any man, but Manuel Africa, García's spy inside the Roja cartel.

Large nails had been used to secure Africa's wrists and ankles to the cross. His head was up, roped there with some cord, and a sign hung across his bloodied chest. It read, *Muerte a los traidoros.*

That was when Sergeant Velasco spoke. "Somebody's been

digging holes around here, Captain. Look... There, there, and there."

García looked, and sure enough, patches of darker soil marked the spots where the digging had taken place. *Why?*

A chill ran down García's spine. He thumbed his radio. *¡Corran! ¡Cúbrete entre las rocas!*"

But it was too late to take cover. As the soldiers scattered, so-called "Jumping Jack" mines shot up out of the ground to a height of approximately four feet, where they exploded and hurled ball bearings in every direction.

The overlapping zones of death cut dozens of soldiers down, including García, who was struck in the back. Then, as the officer tried to disappear, a machinegun opened fire from the top of the bank. He was praying when the bullets found him.

Ricardo and Benito Ayo were lying side-by-side when they triggered the mines. The Jumping Jacks were new to them, and were quite expensive, but oh, what a sight!

Sheets of blood flew, soldados danced like marionettes, and the steady *bang, bang, bang* was reminiscent of Dia de los Muertos when the firecrackers came out. The machine gun fire was like dessert.

"Damn," Ricardo said, as he got to his feet. "That was a sight to see. Francisco! Get wide shots from up here. Then go down and shoot closeups. I want to own the evening news."

Benito felt a jab of jealousy. Why was Ricardo giving the orders? And shouldn't he say "we?" As in, "We want to own the evening news." It was his idea after all.

It was a small thing. But a lot of small things can add up to a big thing. And it was eating at Benito.

Once the photography was over the Reds went down to create a helipad by dragging bodies out of the way. Then a distant buzz was heard, a dot turned into a four-place helicopter, and dust flew as it landed.

The downdraft was sufficient to blow what remained of the cross over, taking Manuel Africa's body with it, adding another corpse to those scattered all around.

The brothers were airborne minutes later. "Mother would be proud," Ricardo shouted.

Benito was silent.

Days passed. And, when Ricardo left for business meetings in Mexico City, Benito was left to fuss and fume. But there was nothing he could do so long as his brother was in charge. So, Benito drank, rode his horse, and issued orders to the servants. None of whom needed his guidance.

When Mayor Aguilar arrived, Benito was seated behind his mother's desk, watching cartoons on the wall-mounted TV. A servant arrived with the news. "Mayor Aguilar is here to see Ricardo. Should I send him away?"

Benito frowned. "Aguilar? Who the hell is he?"

"The Mayor of Lugar de Paz, sir."

"Oh, yes… Lugar de Paz. What does he want?"

"He claims to have information about the man who killed your mother," the servant answered patiently. "He wants the reward."

"¡Mierda! Why didn't you say so? Show him in."

The man who entered was short, balding, and dressed in a cheap suit. He was holding a straw hat which he had rotated counter clockwise.

Benito could be charming when he chose to be, and went forward to shake hands. "Mayor Aguilar! Welcome to Hacienda Roja. My name is Benito Ayo. Please, have a seat."

*

Aguilar managed a weak smile. He was well aware of the fact that Benito was also known as El Niño, and reportedly responsible for countless murders.

But, if he wanted to collect the twenty-five thousand dollar reward offered for information related to the person or persons responsible for the murder of Elena Isabella Ayo, he had to enter the lion's den. And, rather than Ricardo Ayo, he was about to deal with the notorious younger brother. "Thank you, Señor… You are most gracious."

Aguilar was a sniveling fool. And Benito liked that. He perched on the corner of his mother's desk. "So, I understand that you have information regarding my mother's murder. And that's to say nothing of my brother Mateo. If so, you will be richly rewarded. Please share what you know."

Aguilar's voice quavered as he spoke. "The murderer's name is Nick Serrano. He arrived in Lugar de Paz about six months ago. He has enemies. Lots of enemies. And whenever they come to town, Serrano kills them. He is—how do you say? A pistolero. A few months after Serrano arrived, there was an attack on Rancho del Sol, which is owned by El Cuchillo, and his house burned to the ground."

Benito nodded. "Sí. And?"

"El Cuchillo wanted revenge," Aguilar replied. "And Serrano's novia has a son. So, El Cuchillo kidnapped the boy. Your mother's death was the ransom."

It made sense. All of it made sense. But Benito had to be absolutely sure. "Okay, that's quite a story. But how do I know that Serrano, and the man who killed my mother, are the same person?"

Aguilar swallowed. "According to the rumors, you were

present when your mother was killed. Is that true?"

"Yes," Benito replied darkly. "It's true."

"I have a photo of Nick Serrano," Aguilar said. "It's in my pocket."

"Go ahead and take it out," Benito said. "Slowly."

Aguilar made a show out of opening his suit jacket, reaching in, and removing a creased photo. Benito went forward to receive it. The photo was a tight shot of a man with even features, and two days' worth of stubble, looking off camera.

Benito felt something akin to an electric shock surge through his body. It was him! The man who murdered his mother. There was no fucking doubt about it.

Benito wanted to scream obscenities, cry, and dance for joy all at the same time. It took all his strength to remain outwardly calm. "Thank you, Mayor Aguilar. Please wait here. I will return with your reward."

All Aguilar could do was to wait. His hands were shaking, and for good reason. El Niño had what he wanted. Why pay? When he could kill the informer instead?

Aguilar was gambling his life and knew it. But twenty-five thousand was a lot of money... And he'd been unable to resist. Plus, there was the matter of his pride. He would never forget the manner in which Serrano had barged into his office and shamed him. His hands trembled. Would Benito return with the dinero? Or would narcos come to take him away?

Aguilar heard footsteps. Benito appeared. He was holding a paper bag. "Here you go, Mayor. Would you like to count it?"

Aguilar stood. All he wanted to do at that point was to leave the hacienda alive. "No, Señor. I trust you."

"And I trust you," Benito said, as he handed the bag over.

"You'll find twelve-thousand, five-hundred dollars in there, along with a cell phone, and a number. Call it if Serrano leaves town. Otherwise, there's no reason to do anything at all. The rest of the money will be delivered to you once Serrano is dead. Do we understand each other?"

Aguilar nodded. "Yes, I understand."

"Good. You can leave."

Benito watched Aguilar go. Twelve-five wasn't a lot of money by cartel standards. But Ricardo would be pissed. *Why?* Because he wanted to make each and every decision. That's why. Well, fuck him. That shit was going to change.

Lugar de Paz, Mexico

The sun was up, the sky was blue, and Nick Serrano was happy. Finally, Mr. Yankovic was dead, and he could enjoy life without having to be constantly on guard.

"You're smiling," Martina observed, as she eyed him over her coffee mug.

They were seated on the tiny patio located next to La Casa Bonita. Paco was playing with Macho. "Of course I'm smiling," Serrano replied. "I'm here with you."

"Yes, you are," Martina said. "And I asked you a question. A mariachi band? Or no mariachi band?"

After returning from the States, Serrano wasted little time asking Martina to marry him. And, following a discussion with her son, she said "Yes."

That was when the seemingly endless questions began. Should the ceremony be held at Father Colon's church? Or at Pancho's restaurant? And who should they invite? A small group of family and friends? Or the whole town?

Now, even though those questions had been answered, Serrano found himself drowning in other minutiae, including who would function as los padrinos y madrinas—a role similar to godparents. As such, they would sponsor parts of the wedding.

And it didn't stop there. What sort of vows would be exchanged? There were wedding rings to consider, and las arras—the coins that would symbolize the couple's commitment to each other. All of which were important to Martina.

"A mariachi band is a must," Serrano assured her. "So people can dance."

That was the correct answer, judging from the warmth of Martina's smile. It felt good to be home.

La Hacienda Roja, Mexico

The Ortegos cartel controlled a broad swath of land that stretched from Puerto Vallarta in the west to Veracruz in the east, with the Ayo clan's holdings to the north of that.

Which was to say that, had the Ortegos chosen to, they could have gone to war with the Las Rojas cartel and won. That's what Ricardo feared, and why he'd agreed to a conferencia to discuss the possibility of an alliance. And not just an alliance, but the first step toward a narco state which would embrace all of Mexico. The very thing that his father had dreamed of.

Benito, on the other hand, was of the opinion that Ricardo was agreeing too quickly. "Negotiations haven't begun," the younger brother complained, "and you're caving in. Is that what mother would have done? I don't think so."

But Ricardo's mind was made up. "Mother didn't fight battles she couldn't win," he countered. "Pack a bag. We're going to Lake Chapala."

Lake Chapala was located five hours east of Puerto Vallarta, covered 420 miles, and was quite shallow. It was surrounded by low mountains blanketed with greenery, and fed by three rivers.

Chapala was a relatively small city of 51,000 residents, and was known for its good shopping and active nightlife. That made it the ideal location for the Ortego family's sprawling lakeside retreat called Sueño Diurno.

Although there was nothing dreamlike about the armed narcos who met the Ayo brothers at the airport, or the gun trucks that accompanied their armored limo into the Ortegos' walled compound.

That too was fortified and defended by uniformed "retainers" who were clearly a cut above the unkempt rabble that served lesser cartels.

As for the Ortegos themselves, they came across as socialites rather than the iron-fisted drug dealers they actually were. There was Harvard graduate Jorge, the tennis-playing leader of the clan, plus his beauty queen-wife Serena, and their two teenaged daughters. Both of whom had a haughty demeanor.

Once introductions were complete, Ricardo and Benito were led to a two-bedroom guest suite which looked out over the sparkling lake. "This is the way to live," Ricardo observed. "Who knows? If we do a deal, we could buy land and build a retreat."

Benito bit his tongue. It seemed safe to assume that the suite was bugged. But the Ortegos couldn't hear his thoughts, which were rebellious, to say the least. He was of the opinion that rather than play pattycake with the Ortegos, it would be preferable to invade Lugar de Paz and find Nick Serrano. Then, once the murderer was dead and the village was reduced to smoking ruins, they could court the Ortegos.

But Ricardo disagreed. "We can have our revenge any day

of the week. But the opportunity to meet with the Ortegos is something special."

Dinner was a formal affair. And, thanks to the training received from their mother, the brothers were able to choose the correct silverware for each course, tell self-effacing stories, and occasionally highlight their accomplishments—the so-called "777 Ambush" being one of them.

"Yes," Jorge said, as he patted his lip with a linen napkin. "That was brilliant! And sending video to key news outlets was pure genius. Which one of you thought of that?"

The video had been Benito's brainchild, and he was about to say as much, when Ricardo beat him to it. "That was my idea, Jorge. We're fighting two wars... One to take and hold ground. The other is aimed at winning the hearts and minds of the people."

Benito felt a surge of resentment as the Ortegos clapped, Ricardo beamed, and their desserts arrived. Benito ate. But the taste was anything but sweet.

The next day was spent discussing the many difficulties that they would have to overcome in order to supplant the Mexican government, especially how other cartels would react, since they were a good deal more dangerous than any army unit.

Ricardo took the lead during the discussions, leaving Benito to fume, so that by the end of the day he could barely contain his rage.

Ricardo knew his brother was pissed and didn't care. For this reason, there was very little talk on the way to the airport, or during the subsequent flight.

After landing at Hacienda Roja, the brothers exited the plane and made their way toward the house. Ricardo was leading the way when Benito drew a nine-millimeter pistol, took aim, and shot his brother in the head.

The report was quite loud, and half-a-dozen security people responded. "It was him!" Benito shouted. "The man who murdered my mother! Find him!"

Staff ran in every direction. Benito knelt next to the body. Tears were running down his cheeks. And they were tears of joy.

Chapter Fifteen

Lugar de Paz, Mexico

Diego and Carlos were carrying a great deal of weight on their backs. Some real and some perceived. There was the dynamite, yes, but more than that, the responsibility for striking the first blow.

Benito Ayo had stressed that. "We're going to attack Lugar de Paz and find the man who killed my mother and brother. And you will lead the way! According to what my spies tell me, Lugar de Paz has a well-trained guerilla force which stands ready to defend the town from scum like El Cuchillo. But their organization has a weak point. Because of a shortage of funds, they've been forced to rely on cellphones for communications, rather than radios. If we destroy their cell tower before the attack, they'll be unable to coordinate their defense. And that's where you come in. By sneaking into town at night, and planting explosives at the base of the tower, you can bring it down. Once that's accomplished, you can leave town and return here."

As one of the Ayo family's most trusted retainers, Diego was adept at reading subtext. And Benito's message was clear: *Destroy the tower and you can return to the safety of the hacienda without being part of the bloodbath in Lugar de Paz.* So, Diego had a strong incentive to say, "Yes." Which he did.

And, because Carlos trusted Diego, he said, "Yes," as well.

And that was how the two men wound up transporting packs filled with explosives to the Place of Peace.

Lookouts were stationed in Lugar de Paz at night. That's what Benito's spies had reported. But only a couple of them. And because they were old, and creaky, they had a tendency to remain close to their homes. Neither of which were located near the cell tower.

And, since the lookouts lacked the means to stop vehicles and search them, the best way to enter town had been in the back of a van.

Once it stopped, the men jumped out and hurried to enter the deep shadows. The van was already in motion by then. The whole thing was accomplished so quickly that the lookouts were unlikely to have taken notice, even if they were tracking the vehicle. "Come," Diego said. "We have work to do."

Nick Serrano was awoken by the sound of an explosion, and knew what it meant. Insurgents were attacking his outpost again. Had they been able to penetrate the perimeter? That was unlikely, but not impossible.

Serrano grabbed a revolver and stood. That was when he remembered where he was—it was a dream then. Or was it? Serrano heard the wail of the town's single fire engine and knew the answer. He was awake and something bad had occurred.

Serrano's first instinct was to call store owner, Manuel Mendoza, the man in charge of the town's volunteer lookouts. But when Serrano thumbed his phone, he couldn't call out. And then it hit him—the cell tower. The fucking cell tower! It was and always had been the town's Achilles heel. If it had been destroyed, the phone-tree warning system was off line. And who would want to take Lugar de Paz down? El Cuchillo, that's who. Serrano hurried to put his clothes on.

Martina Blanco looked at her clock. It was 3:37 on the morning of her wedding day. Paco came running into her room. "Mamá! Something went *boom!*"

Martina realized that he was right. Something had gone *boom*. But what? She checked her phone for text messages. Nada.

It soon became apparent that everything was down. Text, email, *and* phone. Church bells began to chime. The backup warning system! Lugar de Paz was under attack.

Martina felt a surge of fear. "Get dressed Paco, and grab your emergency backpack. This isn't a drill."

Benito Ayo was ecstatic. The tower was down, a secondary fire was burning, and his ejército de retribución was about to enter Lugar de Paz. The army consisted of one hundred seven men, ten armed vehicles, and yes—a helicopter! Engines roared and rotors clattered as the helo passed over El Niño's Humvee and approached the town. And more than that… Nick Serrano's home. Mayor Aguilar's hand-drawn map was Benito's guide. It was clutched in his hand.

As a parishioner rang the bells, Father Colon greeted the first file of children at the front door of his church, and blessed each one. Teenagers then led each group down into the only basement that the town of Lugar de Paz had. All except Paco Blanco that is, who managed to slip away, and lose himself in shadows.

With his emergency go-bag in back, Serrano drove the Chevrolet Silverado downhill. The bed was loaded with gravel, which made it heavy and difficult to steer. A fire was burning off to the right, near the spot where the cell tower had been, and he figured it was the hotel.

Serrano arrived at the end of main street just seconds after Señor Flores, who was getting out of his dump truck. He was armed with a lever action Winchester, and wearing a cartridge belt worthy of Pancho Villa.

Serrano pulled into position so that the pickup and the larger truck were back-to-back, an arrangement that would make it that much more difficult for the enemy to crash through. They shook hands. "Buena suerte," Flores said.

"You, too," Serrano replied. "Take cover… This is the real thing."

Flores nodded soberly. "It will be like the Mexican Revolution."

Serrano hoped that Flores was wrong, because the Mexican Revolution was a ten-year-long shit show. But he smiled and nodded. "¡Viva México!"

Even though cell service had been lost, the guerillas knew what to do. *If we lose contact with each other, we'll abandon the centralized command-and-control structure, and operate as autonomous teams. Each team will have a leader, and each leader will have a specific assignment.* That's what the fighters had been taught, and Serrano felt certain that they were acting accordingly.

His five-person team consisted of store owner Manuel Mendoza, beautician María López, garage owner Carlos Alonso, undertaker Tomás Pérez, and carpenter Luis Garza. Their responsibility was to defend the steel bridge on the west side of town.

Once across it, attackers could take a right at the foot of the tank, and cruise down main street, killing and looting. Serrano began to run. The town's lights illuminated some spots and threw shadows over others.

A helicopter roared overhead, hovered, and blew dust every which way as a gunner opened fire with a light machine gun. Serrano zigged and zagged, as bullets splattered around him. That was when a hand grenade fell, bounced, and exploded. Shrapnel flew, and Serrano felt something nip his neck, as he ducked behind a parked car.

The vehicle shivered as bullets struck it and Serrano opened the go-bag. The M27 Infantry Automatic Rifle was loaded and ready to fire.

Serrano was reminded of the Rojas' hacienda, and the helo he'd been forced to confront there. *Same song, different verse,* Serrano thought to himself, as he waited for the aircraft to complete a full rotation. Then, with the canopy in his sight, he fired.

Martina and her team were responsible for defending the local health clinic, which was under fire when Paco scooted in. Martina was both angry and relieved. "Paco! You're supposed to be in the church."

"I don't want to hide, Mamá; I want to help," Paco declared.

Martina couldn't send him back to the church on his own and couldn't leave her team. "Alright, son… Collect empty magazines and reload them. You know how, right?"

"You taught me."

Martina sighed. "Yes, I did. Keep your head down."

A rocket hit the building, a wall crumbled, and people screamed.

Benito Ayo's Humvee jerked to a halt and everyone got out. "There!" Benito said, as he pointed. "That's the house. If you find a man in there, take him alive. Go!"

There were three narcos. Benito watched them approach the house, and heard the sound of barking, followed by a shot. "Dog down," the team leader said laconically.

Benito heard a bang as his men kicked the door in, but no gunfire, suggesting that Serrano wasn't home. Because he sure as hell wasn't asleep. Not with all the noise.

Benito's driver, a man named Vega, fell forward onto his face. An arrow was protruding from his back. Fortunately for Benito, he had the presence of mind to throw himself forward. A second arrow whispered through the air above him.

"No one's home," the team leader announced.

"Scan the area before you exit," Benito said. "Vega took an arrow in the back."

Things were not going as planned.

The Church of John the Warrior was sealed. All the doors were locked. The children were in the basement. And the bells continued to toll as someone hammered on the front door. With a rifle butt? Probably.

Father Colon turned to the altar. "Forgive me, Lord, I am about to sin. Not for myself, but for the children, *your* children."

And with that Colon turned to face the entrance. Wood splintered. And, when the door slammed open, Colon fired the twelve-gauge shotgun.

The first narco through the door was thrown backward into those behind him. A parishioner named Díaz fired into the crowd. He was praying out loud.

"Yea, though I walk through the valley of the shadow of death, I will fear no evil: for thou art with me, and I have an AR-15."

Father Colon fired, and fired again. The last narco fell. Colon crossed himself. "Thank you, Lord. Come, Señor Díaz. Help me block the door."

The helicopter was a big target. Serrano fired a burst. But the bullets had no visible effect. And the machine veered away.

Serrano turned and ran toward the bridge. He could hear the constant chatter of automatic fire, interspersed with the boom of exploding grenades, and knew his team was outgunned.

The sky was lighter by then… That, plus the burning Humvee, served to illuminate the scene on the bridge deck. Another Hummer was easing forward in the second lane, machine gun blazing, as it squeezed past the wreck.

That was when Serrano noticed the red flag drooping from the vehicle's antenna. The attackers weren't fighting for El Cuchillo… They were aligned with Las Rojas! And were determined to get revenge for Elena Ayo and her son Mateo.

Serrano dashed across the highway, took cover behind a bullet-riddled truck, and began to fire short bursts. The second Hummer kept coming. Mendoza appeared next to him. "I'm sorry, Jefe. We lost López and Garza."

Serrano winced. "Damn it. We've got to pull back."

"They'll pour into town."

"Yeah," Serrano said. "I know. Bring Pérez and Alonso in. We'll try to slow them down. That's the best we can do."

Narcos tried to enter the clinic and were repulsed by Martina and the others.

Doctor Villar ignored the furor as she hurried to clamp a bleeder. "Get some normal saline and a suture kit. We've got to get his pressure back up."

Martina felt a rising sense of fear. The guerillas were losing the battle. She could feel it. Should the townspeople surrender? Fuck, no. Martina feared that they would be slaughtered. Men, women, and children.

She glanced at Paco. He was hiding under a table methodically loading cartridges into magazines. Martina bit her lower lip. Then she turned back to the shattered window. "Get ready! Here they come!"

Benito was winning and he knew it. That was good. But the real prize had escaped him. Serrano… Where the hell was Serrano?

Benito thumbed his radio. "Ortiz… Where is the worst fighting?"

Ortiz was El Niño's second in command. "Our guys are still trying to break into the church, and a lot of fighters are holed up in the restaurant. But the health clinic is the worst. There's a rifleman in every window."

That's it, Benito thought. *A man like Serrano will be where the fighting is fiercest.* He turned to his men. "Follow me! We'll end this."

Father Colon was out of breath by the time he reached the top of the steeple's stairs. A parishioner named Nina was waiting. It was hard for the girl to make herself heard over the church bells. "A convoy is approaching, Father! Look!"

Colon accepted the binoculars and looked to the south. Nina was right. He could see vehicles with flags flying. More Rojas? No. The flags weren't red.

Colon waited for a flag to flap open, saw the dagger symbol, and could hardly believe his eyes. El Cuchillo's narcos were arriving from the south. But to do *what?*

The answer was obvious. The Rojas were on what Ramirez considered to be his turf! And, after the attack on his home, The Knife was determined to retaliate. He turned to Nina. "Find Serrano! Find Martina! Tell them that El Cuchillo is about to attack the Rojas. Hurry!"

The inside of the health clinic resembled a charnel house. The wounded and the dead lay side by side as Doctor Villar and her assistants sought to save as many people as they could.

Martina had given up hope. Only a handful of defenders remained on their feet and they were running out of ammunition. Maybe they should surrender. Maybe the Rojas would be merciful. Martina smiled crookedly. And maybe pigs would fly.

A wall collapsed as a Humvee struck it and more narcos flooded in. The man who led them shouted. "Drop your weapons! Give us Nick Serrano. That's all we want. Is he here?"

That confirmed what Martina already suspected. The Rojas were after revenge. For Elena Ayo's death and that of her middle son. And they knew Serrano was responsible.

Martina was reminded of what Serrano had done for Paco. For her.

Martina stepped forward with her rifle pointed at the blood smeared floor. "No. He isn't here. Are you the one they call *El Niño?*"

The man stared at her. Martina could see the madness in his eyes. "Yes."

"Then you should run," Martina told him. "Serrano will kill you for this."

Benito began to raise his weapon. "Perhaps. But you'll be dead."

That's when Martina heard a bang, and saw a hole appear between Benito's eyes.

A second shot followed the first, and was only a quarter of an inch off. The last member of the Ayo family collapsed.

Martina raised her rifle, and the others did as well, causing Benito's narcos to back away. Fighting for Benito was one thing. But fighting for a dead man was stupid.

Martina turned to look at Paco. He was standing there, holding the .22 with both hands, ready to fire again. "If they're worth one, they're worth two," the little boy said. "That's what Nick says. Right, Mamí?" Martina began to cry.

Word of El Niño's death spread quickly by radio, causing his fighters to flee. Or try to flee, because El Cuchillo's narcos were blocking all the exit routes, and immediately opened fire.

The Rojas fought back. But after losing both Benito and Ortiz—who'd been killed near the church—they were little more than a mob. Most surrendered. Those who refused were shot.

Benito's helicopter circled the town, took fire, and fled south.

Serrano found Ramirez standing on the hood of an ex-army Panhard VBL, shouting at people. "Search the prisoners! Take their weapons. Check IDs."

When Ramirez saw that his men were pointing weapons at Serrano, he ordered, "Leave El Soldado alone." Then he jumped to the ground. "We meet again."

"Yes," Serrano replied. "You intervened. Why?"

Ramirez shrugged. "Lugar de Paz lies within *my* territory. And the Rojas attacked my home. That's reason enough."

"What will you do with the prisoners?"

"I will hire some of them," Ramirez said. "And free the rest."

"*Free* them?" Serrano inquired incredulously. "They're murderers. Thieves at best."

Ramirez frowned. "What would you have me do? Turn them in to the government? Lock them in imaginary prisons? Slaughter them? No, I refuse to do any of those things. What I *will* do is march them out of town for you."

That, Serrano decided, was better than nothing. "Are you going to seize the Ayo hacienda?"

Ramirez shook his head. "I predict that the Ortegos will take control of it. They want to create a narco state, and will use their political clout to acquire the Ayo hacienda and the rest of the family holdings. I lack the means to stop them."

Serrano nodded. "Don't come back here, Señor Ramirez."

"Don't give me cause, Señor Serrano. I understand that today is your wedding day. Congratulations. Martina Blanco is a fine woman. And her son is a good boy. I wish you peace and serenity." And with that El Cuchillo turned his back and walked away.

It was, Serrano decided, a wedding present of sorts.

Chapter Sixteen

Lugar de Paz, Mexico

The wedding, when it occurred, was thirty days late. The funerals were over by then, for townspeople and narcos alike, and most of the battle-related debris had been removed.

Repairs were underway at Pancho's restaurant, the health clinic, and the bank—all of which had been hit hard. As for the cell tower, a new one was being assembled, and would be functional soon.

The vows took place in the church, and were presided over by Father Colon, who relished the recitations, songs, and blessings that led up to the exchange of consent—and the giving of rings.

The concluding rites were followed by a processional that led to Pancho's, and a party complete with food, drinks, and a mariachi band. The whole town had been invited. And most of the citizens were in attendance.

Finally, after retreating to La Casa Bonita and putting Paco to bed, the newlyweds went out to the patio where they sipped drinks, held hands, and discussed the future. It was bright.

Martina would teach, and continue to sing, while Serrano supervised construction of a larger house. And after that? Time would tell.

*

Mayor Aguilar was found three days later, slumped over the wheel of his brand-new car, with a bullet hole in his back. A note was pinned to his jacket. It read: "For those who died to protect the Place of Peace." A culprit was never identified.

About the Author

William C. Dietz is the bestselling author of more than sixty novels, some of which have been translated into German, Russian, and Japanese.

He grew up in the Seattle area, served as a medic with the Navy and Marine Corps, graduated from the University of Washington, and has been employed as a surgical technician, college instructor, and producer. Prior to becoming a full-time writer, Dietz served as director of public relations and marketing for an international telephone company.

For more about William C. Dietz and his fiction, or to contact him, please visit williamcdietz.com.

You can also connect with him on Facebook at: www.facebook.com/williamcdietz.